Frederick C. Brewster

From Independence Hall Around the World

Volume 1

Frederick C. Brewster

From Independence Hall Around the World
Volume 1

ISBN/EAN: 9783337193959

Printed in Europe, USA, Canada, Australia, Japan

Cover: Foto ©Andreas Hilbeck / pixelio.de

More available books at **www.hansebooks.com**

FROM

INDEPENDENCE HALL

AROUND THE WORLD

BY

F. CARROLL BREWSTER, LL.D.

PHILADELPHIA:
THE LEVYTYPE COMPANY.
1895.

PUBLISHER'S PREFACE.

Nowadays, when the facilities of travel on the one hand, and of publication on the other, have made both a voyage around the globe and the printing of its narrative a common-place matter, there is need of something in the way of an apology for the bringing out of another book of this kind.

Apart from the fact that Judge Brewster's notes of his journey, originally made only as private memoranda, have been published in response, primarily, to many requests to that end, a broader reason for the present work will be found by the reader in the freshness and simplicity of the voyager's recital, in its freedom from the conventional spirit of traveler's tales, in its pointed expression of unbiased views regarding the places and the peoples that he describes. The chronicle of Judge Brewster's journey is clearly that of a keen observer, whose considerations are the reflections of a disciplined mind, whose statements are those of an unprepossessed reporter, and whose narrative is presented as a simple and unvarnished tale.

In collating the illustrations for this journey

around the world, the publishers have supplemented the pictures collected by Judge Brewster with a number selected from other sources, and desire here to note their indebtedness to Stuart Culin, Esq., Director of the Archæological Department of the University of Pennsylvania, for copies of the ethnological illustrations of the Museum, and to Simon A. Stern, Esq., for the use of the extensive series of photographs collected by him on the occasion of his mission to the Chinese government.

L. E. L.

Philadelphia, June, 1895.

TABLE OF CONTENTS.

TABLE OF CONTENTS

PREFACE.

THE narrative of a tour of the world should be written by one who combines the learning of the historian, the geographer, the astronomer, the statistician, the student of architecture, painting, statuary and all the arts.

The work would then be worthy of the study of all men, for it would edify, instruct, enlighten and delight the reader.

Time should also be devoted to the journey, for the faithful examination of every temple, mosque, tomb, gallery and object of research and of study.

When the author of this brochure recollects that he possesses none of the mental qualifications above referred to, and that he could not devote the necessary time for the examination of places visited, he feels as if he owed most ample excuse for attempting to publish his reminiscences. The truth is his apology. He travelled in a hurry and wrote as opportunity permitted some hasty memoranda of his journeys. He was requested to publish his manuscript, and he has not had time to re-write or to extend it. Such as it is, and with its many imperfections he reluctantly hands it to the printer.

The journeys here described occupied four months and thirteen days. Deducting for a stay in California, four months may be said to represent the actual time employed. Continents, seas, oceans are crossed, and much is seen in such a span of days, but it leaves no time for thorough examination or for needed rest. Egypt, Palestine, Turkey, Greece and all the important cities of Europe were omitted on this excursion and a feverish anxiety to return home pushed the traveller from Port Said to Brindisi, then across Italy, France, and the Atlantic to the United States.

INTRODUCTION.

THE first man known to history as attempting to circumnavigate the world was Ferdinand Magellan. He sailed from San Lucar in 1519, went to South America, passed through the straits to which he gave his name, and up the Pacific ocean to the Phillipine Islands. There he was unfortunately killed in 1521, in a conflict with the natives. His vessel however returned in safety to Spain September 6, 1522, thus making the first voyage round the world.

Sir Francis Drake is the next historical celebrity in this connection. He was the first Englishman to attempt a voyage around the world. He commenced his celebrated expedition at 32 years of age.

The best portrait of him extant pictures him as of middle height, with brown hair, high forehead, long grey eyes, small ears, and a long moustache and beard covering his mouth and chin. He is dressed in a loose dark shirt, with a belt around his waist.

He sailed from Plymouth, England on the Pelican, of only 120 tons, November 15, 1577. He had with him four other vessels, one of fifty, one of thirty and two of eighty tons. His whole force consisted of 166 men. The Pelican carried twenty guns. His destination was unknown to his crew. Shortly after sailing, a storm overtook him, which compelled a return to Falmouth for repairs. He started again December 13, went to the Cape de Verde Islands; after robbing a few Spanish vessels, he sailed to South America. In this neighborhood one of his captains, Doughty, deserted; search was made for him, he was captured and transferred with his crew to the Pelican. Drake then proceeded to Patagonia, where Doughty was tried, condemned to death, and was beheaded.

After three weeks of hardship the navigators found themselves in the Pacific. There remained only the Pelican, the Elizabeth and the thirty ton cutter. The cutter went down in a hurricane.

The captain of the Elizabeth left Drake and reached England in the following June. Drake remained. He soon met an Indian fisherman who informed him of a galleon in the harbor of Valparaiso. The Pelican sailed alongside her prize, and surprised the Spanish seamen. Not caring to injure them, Drake seized their treasures. Silver of the value of four thousand ducats was transferred to the Pelican. Drake also robbed the "Cacafuego" which was laden with all the bullion of the season's mining, gold and jewels, on her way from the Isthmus. The full value of all his plunder remained a secret between Drake and the Queen.

Near the coast of Mexico the Pelican plundered a Chinese vessel, and robbed the principal citizens of a Spanish settlement. In lower California a mouth was spent repairing the Pelican. April 16, 1579, Drake started north in hope of finding a northern passage. Before the summer was ended, England and Spain had learned of Drake's plunderings.

Phillip wrote to England to be instantly informed of the pirates arrival, and requested the restoration of the plunder and the punishment of the offender. He also sent ships to guard the straits of Magellan. Drake stopped at San Francisco, and secured the good graces of the Indians by presenting them with medicines and ointments. They believed him to be a god, and offered sacrifice to him.

During his stay he discovered the existence of gold. Setting sail again, he passed along the Java coast and came near being stranded. A change of wind brought his ship into deep water, and proceeding westward he passed through the straits of Sunda, reaching Plymouth in October. Not having heard of Drake for eighteen months, the whole country rang with his praises. The Queen was delighted and received him with great honor.

The Spanish Ambassador sent word to the Queen that unless restoration was made, immediate war must be expected. Fearing she might have to yield, she refused to allow the plunder to be registered, and resolved to reserve a goodly portion for herself, for her favorites, and ten thousand pounds for Drake and his company. She sent Drake to Plymouth to take charge of the booty, and selected a magistrate on whom she could rely to inventory the cargo, allowing Drake time and opportunity for removing a great part of the plunder before registration was made.

On Drake's return to London, he was received with great favor, the Queen bestowing upon him the honor of knighthood. He was however censured by men whose good opinion he valued, and he gave them handsome presents in the hope of changing this opposition. He presented a diamond cross with a crown set with enormous emeralds to the Queen. She wore this on New Year's day.

Burghley and Sussex, to their honor be it said, would not accept the presents of the pirate.

Captain Cook's name is known to every school boy. He made three successful voyages round the world.

The first in 1768 was in a small ship, the "Endeavour," of only 370 tons. Diminutive as was this vessel she seems to have been a giantess when compared with the "Santa Maria" of Columbus, which was not over 100 tons.

Cook reached Otaheite or Tahite, where he erected an observatory and made astronomical observations.

From there he sailed in quest of the great continent, then supposed to exist in the South Pacific, and reached the Islands of New Zealand. Owing to the hostility of the natives, he could not penetrate to the interior, and contented himself with a voyage of six months around the coast. He then proceeded to Australia and sighted Botany Bay April 28th. From Australia he sailed to New Guinea and thence to Batavia, where his ship had to put in for repairs.

He arrived in England June 11, 1771, was raised by the King to the rank of Captain, and was placed in command of the "Resolution," a ship of 462 tons, and a smaller ship called the "Adventure." He sailed from Plymouth July 13, 1772, to discover the great southern continent. He reached Madeira July 29, and touched the Cape of Good Hope. January 17, 1773 he sailed for New Zealand and returned to England July 30, 1774. He sailed from Nore June 25, 1776, cruised in the South Pacific, discovered the Sandwich Islands (named after the Earl of Sandwich) and reached America in March, 1778. Returning to winter in the Sandwich

Islands, he discovered Hawaii, where he met his tragical death February 14, 1779.

Many have supposed that Marco Polo sailed round the world. This is a mistake. He was a native of Venice. In April, 1271, at the age of 17, he travelled through Persia and Turkestan, and passing across the great Gobi desert he reached Cathay (China). There he visited Kublai Khan at his summer palace in Shandu. He spent a year with the Khan, learned the language, and wore the Tartar costume.

He became Envoy to the Khan, and at 23 was sent to the western and southern provinces. Among other places he visited Thibet, Nankin, Pekin, and spent considerable time in Kinsai, which was noted for its fine buildings and public baths, of which he found 4000 in the city. He described the women of Kinsai as "of angelic beauty." He returned to Kambalu, where he was welcomed and held in high favor by the Khan. Later, he was sent on another expedition to the Japanese Islands. He describes Ceylon as the loveliest island in the Eastern Seas. Here he saw the jagged mountain called "Adam's Peak" upon which is said to be the tomb of the founder of the Buddhist religion.

As the Envoy of the Khan, he was admitted into the higher class of Hindoos, known as Brahmins. After travelling in the interior of India, he crossed the Indian Ocean toward the coast of Africa and proceeded to the great island of Madagascar, passing through Zanzibar and Abyssinia. He then returned to Kambalu. Sixteen years had now passed since Marco had left his native city. His mission to Cathay had been accomplished. He reported that he had converted the Khan and many of his subjects to Christianity. Marco was 41 years of age when he returned to Venice. Soon after, he enlisted for the war between Genoa and Venice. He commanded a galley, fought bravely, but was captured. His brave commander, Dandola, killed himself rather than be carried a prisoner to Genoa. Marco was imprisoned and occupied the cell with a great scholar of Pisa. They became fast friends. While in prison, he wrote the thrilling story of his travels. Five months later, Marco's father, Nicolo, and his brother, Maffeo, visited him in prison. They offered a large sum as a ransom. Marco was released. A year later, in 1299, he returned to Venice. Shortly afterwards, he married Donata Loredano, the daughter of a nobleman. He died at the age of 70. His travels read like fairy tales.

FROM SAN FRANCISCO (N. 37° 47′)
To HONOLULU (N. 21° 18′)

Distance, 2092 miles.
Time, 6 days, 15 hours.
Fare, 1st class, $100.

DIFFERENCE IN TIME:
Philadelphia, 12 Noon.
San Francisco, 9 A. M.
Honolulu, 6.30 A. M.

VOYAGES on the Pacific are not marked by the number of vessels one generally sees in crossing the Atlantic. A steamer and a sailer were all the ships sighted in six days. A few flying-fish and birds hardly relieved the monotony.

The entrance to the harbor of Honolulu is very picturesque, but it is narrow and dangerous. It is well marked by buoys. Very effective dredging has been done on the bar.

The Hawaiian Republic consists of six large and two small islands; in all, nearly 7000 square miles and 90,000 inhabitants. Honolulu, the capitol, contains a population of about 27,000. The

16

form of government is Republican. The streets of
Honolulu are smooth and well laid out. A tram
connects the centre of the town with the suburbs.
There are some very fine buildings. The largest
was formerly the royal palace. It is now the seat
of government of the Republic. It is of grand
proportions with Corinthian columns. There is a
splendid hospital, a very large stone church, some
smaller places of worship, including a Mormon
chapel. You must add to these the post office,
museum, municipal buildings and many attractive
residences. The appearance, on the whole, is of a
large country town with mountains at the side and
in the rear. A drive of seven miles takes you to
Pali (the cliff), which presents a picture of rare
beauty. Standing upon a shelf of rock some 2000
feet high, you see a perpendicular descent touching
a valley of 1000 acres dotted with two villages and
washed by the ocean. The effect is very grand.
The Island is about sixteen miles on its longest line
and was stated to be over sixty-four miles around.
Tropical trees and plants abound. The date, cocoa-
palm, sorghum, mango, guava, banyan, eucalyptus
(called here kora), bananas, pine-apples, and other
plants, with beautiful flowers, are seen in great pro-
fusion.

The history of these interesting islands, since their
first discovery by Cook, is well known. The arrival

of our missionaries in 1820 and 1823 was followed
by the conversion of the Queen and of all the king-
dom.

Vancouver is credited with the introduction of
cattle and of chickens. The best horses are brought
from the United States. A splendid grey was
quoted at $250.

Subsequent to Vancouver's last visit and prior to
the conquest
by Kameha-
meha, t h e
harbor of
Honolulu
was discov-
ered by Cap-
tain Brown
of the British
ship Butter-
worth. He
called it Fair-
haven. Sur-
veys followed
by the British and Russians.

GOVERNMENT HOUSE, HONOLULU.

Aside from the conversion of the people to Christianity, there have been several historical items of
some interest in the life of this nation. The first
was in 1843. The British Consul had complained
to Lord George Paulet, commanding the " Carys-

fort," of outrages inflicted upon him and other
subjects of her Majesty. A suit had been brought
for a laundry bill and an attachment had been
issued against certain property. For these and
other wrongs Captain Paulet sent to the King six
demands. The first of these was for the removal of
the odious attachment. This was accompanied by
a threat of bombardment to be carried into effect
the next afternoon.

The King meekly replied that he would comply,
but under protest, and referred the whole question to
her Majesty. But this only emboldened the Captain
to present other demands, and the King in despair
exclaiming that " he would not die piecemeal " and
entering his solemn protest, ceded the islands to
Great Britain, reserving his appeal to her Majesty.
Captain Paulet assumed charge. But the Queen
soon terminated the comedy. In a few months
(July 26, 1843) Admiral Thomas arrived in H. M.
S. Dublin. He immediately sought the King—
restored the sovereignty and saluted the Hawaiian
standard. Of course a feast was given. History
records this interesting occasion in these words:
" There were three long tables, one at the head run-
" ning cross-wise. At this head table His Majesty
" sat, *on the ground,* in native fashion, with the
" Admiral upon his right and the other officers,
" etc.

"Of knives and forks there were not enough to go "round, and a very nimble use of the fingers was *"* made. . . . There was the finely baked pig. *" the roasted dog and* all the variety of the native *"* fish, flesh and fowl and fruits of the islands."

The next chapter of interest records such recent events as to render notice of them almost unnecessary. It stands alone in the history of the United States. The Queen sought in January, 1893, to break the constitution. Her ministers refused to aid her treason. The people peaceably deposed her. Our representative recognized the new Republic. Seventeen other governments followed suit. And then, to our sorrow, the U. S. President exerted every effort to restore this dethroned Queen. Our country was singularly saved from the reproach by the Queen herself who refused to be restored unless she could behead our citizens.

OF THE EXTINCT VOLCANO KILAUEA much has been written by Lady Brassey, Dr. Lyons and others.

A new hotel stands almost on the brink of the crater. The vapors are utilized for baths, etc. The lava floor of the crater is crossed by visitors. It is said that it heaves occasionally and that in 1891 there was a considerable change.

The Following Comparative Table of Nationality of Population of Hawaiian Islands in 1890 may be of Interest:

NATIONALITY.				1890.
Natives	.	.	.	34,436.
Half-castes	.	.	.	6,186.
Chinese	.	.	.	15,301.
Americans	.	.	.	1,928.
Hawaiian born of foreign parents	.			7,495.
Britons	.	.	.	1,344.
Portuguese	.	.	.	8,602.
Germans	.	.	.	1,434.
French	.	.	.	70.
Japanese	.	.	.	12,360.
Norwegian	.	.	.	227.
Other foreigners	.	.	.	419.
Polynesian	.	.	.	588.
				89,990.

OF THE BERNICE PAUAHI BISHOP MUSEUM, W. T. Brigham, A. M., Curator, writes — " That it fulfills two public uses: it preserves in fitting monument the name of one honored and beloved in the community, and it also by its nature and contents adds dignity to the country at large. It was founded in 1889 by Hon. Charles R. Bishop, and placed in the custody of the Trustees of the Kamehameha Schools, with a sufficient endowment to insure its preservation, if not its growth. Externally it is a structure if not perfect architecturally, at least attractive, built of the very bones of the land, the durable lava blocks from one of the

ancient flows that piled up the mountains of Oahu.
Somewhat dark and sombre as this material is, it is
closely covered by the delicate leaves and bright
yellow blossoms of what may be called the ' Honolulu Ivy.' "

Two ample doors in the central tower admit to a
hallway, which, emptied of its ethnological treasures,
would still claim the visitor's attention from the
beauty of the native koa woodwork of the panelled
wainscot and stairs. To the left opens the Kahili
room, finished in white cedar and like the entrance
hall, paved with encaustic tile and brick. On the
other hand is the main room of the museum, above
which and reached by the stairway is the picture
gallery. So much for the general features of this
fire-proof building.

Here it is hoped to collect not only every article
that may illustrate the ethnology of this group, but
also every bird, fish, insect, shell, coral, plant, in
short all that will show in an accurate and
scientific as well as popular way, whatever of life
the islands produce. This must be a work of time
even with the assistance of all the friends of the
museum, but already a beginning has been made,
and experts in the various departments have promised to name the specimens when collected, so that
here in the Pacific may be as accurately named fish,
shells, corals, etc., as can be found in any museum
of Europe or America.

The kahilis head the list of what the museum
has that is not to be found elsewhere, and it has
seemed worth while to attempt to preserve these
rather perishable emblems of royalty.   There are
forty-five of the large processional kahilis and more
than sixty of the smaller fly-brushes.   Some of
these saw the birth of the Kamehameha Dynasty,
others fol-
lowed the last
son of Kame-
hameha I. to
the tomb, and
the latest
made were of
pure white
feathers to
mark the
funeral pomp
of the last of
the Kameha-
mehas, whose

QUEEN STREET, HONOLULU.

name this museum bears.   In the midst of these
impressive kahilis are the Hawaiian birds, and this
collection contains many very choice specimens.   In
the same room are the Niihau mats, one of these
being very old, once the property of Kamehameha
I; another is very large, $14\frac{1}{2}$x$30\frac{1}{2}$ feet.   All of
them are interesting as a manufacture most credit-

2

able to Hawaiian industry, but fast becoming a
lost art.

Of the kapas the museum possesses more than
35,000 square feet, but this immense surface conveys
little idea of the great variety of texture, pattern
and color. All the museums of Europe combined
cannot equal this very remarkable collection, which
fully sustains the reputation of Hawaiian kapas as
the best in the world. In one case in the main
room one can trace the manufacture of bark cloth
from the strip of bark through every process to the
finished product; and better still, examine the texture
of this paper cloth in some 224 specimens placed
like stained glass in the windows.

In wooden bowls and dishes the museum is very
rich, having many of admirable form made long before wood-working machinery was introduced.
These were the "services of plate" of the old kings
and alii. The largest is a bowl nine feet in circumference while the smallest is a little bowl from which
Queen Emma eat in childhood. Here are dishes
for fish, roast pig and dog: finger bowls for washing
at the feast; gourd bottles and cocoanut cups for
drinking; small dishes for inamona, and in the
midst of all these convivial implements to remind
that there is an end to all feasting, like the mummy
of the Egyptian banquet, is the great trough in

which the body of a chief was dissected and his bones cleaned.

The Hawaiians were great fishermen and this handicraft is well shown here. Nets of olona of many kinds, fish traps and hooks of fine workmanship. Of these last some are of human bone, others of tortoise-shell, ivory or sea-shell; and here, too, are the hooks hammered from the nails procured from the early voyagers. The hooks range in size from a tiny shell hook less than half an inch across to the large wooden shark hook that was always baited with human flesh. Among these are the great platters made from alapainui, saturated with the blood of many a slave fatted to make himself useful as shark bait.

Man cannot live to eat and work only; he must have play, and by the playthings here it will be inferred that the old Hawaiians had their share of amusements. Many of these were athletic sports of the finest kind. Would that the youth of the present day could roll the ulumaika with the zest they put into the far inferior base ball; ride the surf-board as easily as they ride the bicycle, and hurl an ihe or spear as powerfully as did the contemporaries of Kamehameha I. Here is a spherical ulu of good workmanship, weighing twenty-two pounds, that would exhaust a modern bowler. But while the men were sliding down hill on the holua, the women

were making feather cloaks or braiding the strands
of human hair for leis in a way far superior to any
other braid of hair found in the Pacific.

Here are Hawaiian adzes in astonishing variety
from the rudely chipped block to the finely finished
tool, and with these are the grind-stones on which

NUUANU STREET—LOOKING UP.

the patient
adz maker
sharpened
the stone.
To go to ex-
tremes we
pass from the
very solid
stone adz,
most durable
of relics, to
an article
which is pro-
verbially
flimsy and ephemeral, a woman's hat. Here are
half a hundred made of a great variety of material
from shavings to bean pods. Those of loulu and
hako are especially fine and suggest the desirability
of a larger manufacture than at present obtains.

Turning from these islands to the more extensive
region that the plan of the museum embraces,
there are several departments where the museum is

as rich as in specimens simply Hawaiian. Of
Maori implements and manufactures there is a re-
markably complete and valuable series. So of Fiji,
while the Marquesas and Society Islands are hardly
represented at all. Micronesia is here in force, so
are New Guinea and Solomon Islands, and there is
a fair show of Australian implements.

In the picture gallery the portraits, although often
far from artistic work, are interesting from their subjects, the Kings, Queens and Alii of Hawaii. The
photographs are very instructive, but strangely, the
poorest of these are those of Hawaiians.

Among the relics is the silver teapot given to
Madame Boki by the King of England, also the one
sent to Kaahumanu, and the large silver cup given
by Queen Victoria to her sister-Queen Emma. Far
more interesting than these is a bit of looking glass
given by Vancouver to Kamehameha I, and which
doubtless has reflected the faces of Hawaii's greatest
chiefs; as if conscious of this it now refuses to re-
flect any more.

HONOLULU'S SYSTEM OF WATER SUPPLY consists of
one intermediate reservoir and three storage basins in
Nuuanu Valley, and one at the entrance of Makiki
Valley (fed by the streams and springs of the neighborhood), with a combined capacity of 40,369,937
gallons, and five flowing artesian wells of seven and

five-eighths inches bore connecting with the mains in the eastern part of the city and Waikiki.

The street mains comprise nearly thirty-six and a half miles of pipe, divided as follows:

One hundred and fifty feet, twenty-four inch; 100 feet, sixteen inch; 10,300 feet, fifteen inch; 27,560 feet, twelve inch; 1000 feet, ten inch; 31,790 feet, six inch; 6220 feet, five inch; 69,574 feet, four inch; 17,285 feet, three inch; 8167 feet, two inch; a total of 192,586 feet.

At the last report of the Superintendent of Water Works for the Legislature of 1892 there were 2109 privileges supplied by the above system, at rates ranging from $5.00 to $320.00 per annum, producing an annual income of over $42,000.

FROM HONOLULU (Lat. 21°, 18′ North)
To YOKOHAMA (Lat. 35°, 26′ North).

Distance, 3420 miles.
Time, 12 days.
Fare, first-class, $100.

DIFFERENCE IN CLOCK :
Philadelphia, 12 Noon.
San Francisco, 9 A. M.
Honolulu, 6.30 A. M.
Yokohama, 2 A. M.

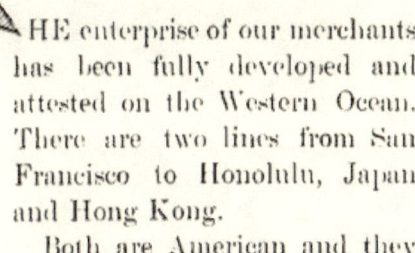

THE enterprise of our merchants has been fully developed and attested on the Western Ocean. There are two lines from San Francisco to Honolulu, Japan and Hong Kong.

Both are American and they work in concert. The Occidental and Oriental have a powerful and celebrated fleet. The Pacific Mail Steamship Company operates the following:

The China, City of Pekin, City of Rio Janeiro, Peru, City of Sydney, Colima Acapulco, Colon, San Blas, San Jose, San Juan, Costa Rica, Starbuck, Barracouta.

Besides these the same Company runs upon the

Atlantic the Newport, City of Para, the Columbia,
and the Miller Griffith (a tug). "The China," the
Queen of the fleet, is 456 feet long, of 5000 tonnage,
and 8000 horse-power. She was built in 1889, at

PILE DWELLINGS AT TOKIO.

Glasgow under the supervision of Captain Wm. B.
Seabury, and cost nearly a million of dollars. Our
country has reason to be proud of Captain Seabury.
He is now in the very prime of life and vigor, although
he has seen thirty-eight years of hard service, twenty-

nine years of which have been with the Pacific M. S.
Company. Think of this sea record: seven times
round Cape Horn before he was 21; nine years in
sailing ships, 101 round voyages from New York to
Colon, fifty six voyages from San Francisco to British
Columbia, five from New York to Sydney, many
from San Francisco to Panama and back and from
San Francisco to China and back one from New
York to San Francisco through the straits of Magellan, one from Glasgow through the Mediterranean
and the Suez Canal to Hong Kong.

THE CLOCK TIME AT SEA.— One does not need to
travel over the sea in order to realize the changes
of the watch.

A journey from Philadelphia to Chicago throws
every time-piece an hour ahead, for noon at the
starting point will be 11 A. M. in the western city.
So if the race with the sun be continued to San
Francisco, the noon of home will become 9 A. M. at
the Pacific. Proceeding on to Honolulu the dis-
crepancy increases, noon of Philadelphia is 6.30 A.
M. at the Sandwich Islands, and at Yokohama the
home mid-day is 2 A. M.

It is clear, therefore, that one can exchange noon
for midnight if he only travel far enough. At that
moment he passes to another day in his calendar.
This is what must be understood by the common
expressions "gaining a day," "losing a day." In

fact, no day is gained nor lost. The day remains,
but by an absolute law of navigation a correction of
time must be made. It was said to the writer that
"out somewhere in the Pacific a day was dropped or
"the same day was twice counted." But the locality

A JINRIKSHAW.

of this "somewhere" and the details of the operation can never be understood, or explained, save by
actual experiment. We all understand that the
circle is marked to contain 360 degrees, whereof 180
degrees are, of course, the half. For the purposes

of navigation most civilized nations calculate from
the meridian of Greenwich. A steamer going west
from Honolulu towards Yokohama may approach
the 180° *west* of Greenwich on her fourth day from

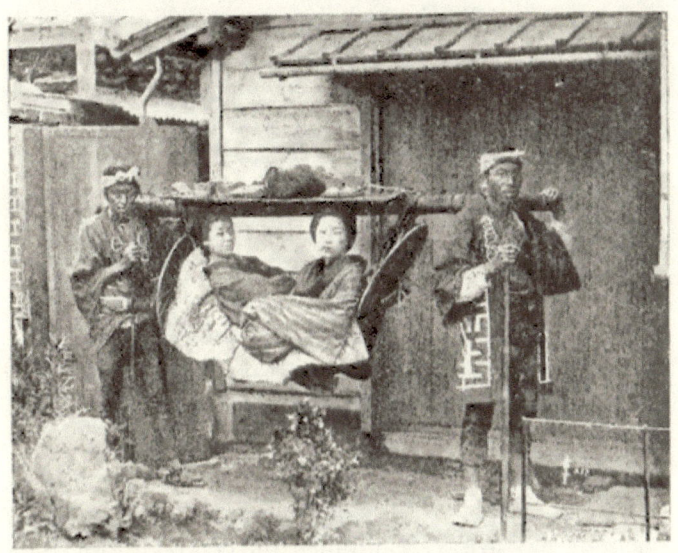

SETTING OUT FOR A JOURNEY IN A "KANGA."

the Sandwich Islands. Suppose that fourth day to
be Saturday, November 18, 1894, and that the 180°
west is crossed at 11 A. M. of that day. As there is
no 181° west, the hour the vessel crosses the line of
180° *west* she finds herself, according to her map
approaching the 179° *east* of Greenwich. Therefore

she must change her day to Greenwich time.   At
Greenwich it is not Saturday, November 18, but
Sunday, November 19, 1894.   The ship accordingly
drops Saturday, calls it Sunday and thus goes on.

An English writer, the celebrated Lieutenant
Leckey, has published a very learned and interesting work entitled "Wrinkles in Practical Navigation."   He explains this somewhat puzzling rule
very clearly: "Going east or west round the world
"there will be no real gain or loss of a day."
Otherwise a man, by continually sailing round east,
might be considered—from the frequent repetition
of a day which it entailed—to have lived longer
than another who stopped at home.   In the case of
the traveller he only *appears* to gain a day, as each
one of those he has lived whilst on his journey has
been shorter by a certain number of minutes which
has arisen from the difference of longitude traversed
between two consecutive arrivals of the sun on his
meridian whilst the day of the man who remained
behind has always contained the complete twenty-
four hours.

Again, if two men, A and B, started at the same
instant on a journey round the world, the first going
east and the other west, and neither made any
alteration in their dates from time of setting out
until their return, together, on the same day, this is
what would happen: A would believe he had

arrived, say on Sunday, and B would persist in considering it as Friday. There would be a difference of two whole days in their reckoning, but no one would seriously entertain the idea that on this account A had lived forty-eight hours longer than B.

The actual day of the week would, of course, be Saturday, and the actual time occupied by each on the journey would be precisely the same."

THE STEERAGE.-The Chinese have a strong attachment for their New Years day, which comes round in February. To guard against the inability of our ships to carry an immense multitude the Orientals start early on their home pilgrimage. Hence in November the Steamship "China" left San Francisco with over 600 Chinese and received 200 more at Honolulu. They pay $51 a head for the voyage from San Francisco to Hong Kong. They sleep on shelves—males separate from females. How they manage to live seems a marvel. The visit to their crowded quarters makes a strong impression on the memory and on the olfactories. The troop is divided into companies of ten. They select a commissary. He obtains a ticket from the steward—presents it when he receives the rations and gets it back when he returns the vessels. There are no tables—no chairs. They sit or squat on the deck, help themselves from the filled tins each commissary brings to his mess by ladling a portion into their cups. Then they eat, laugh and chat in the most contented manner.

The supplies are well cooked and from the avidity with which the articles are consumed they

A JAPANESE RELIGIOUS SERVICE.

must be palatable. But to our eyes the food seems to be curious and unknown. There are three meals served in this fashion per diem. The breakfast is at 7. It consists of beef, cabbage, beans, pickled ginger, orange peel tea. Lunch comes at 12, of shrimps, vermicelli soup, beef, rice, tea. Supper is at 4. It is composed of bean card, cabbage, potatoes and beef stew, dried turnips, salt peas, pickled onions, rice and tea. Sometimes duck eggs are served. These have been preserved in coatings of yellow or black earth. The boast is made that these coverings keep the eggs fresh. But this is not always the result. Nor indeed do all the Chinese so desire it to be. One will take a very rotten egg and refuse it. Another will pick it up, and devour it—saying, "Ah! Ah! Inglee man take cheesee all maggots good in mouth. I likee black eggee."

So forcible is the example of the great!

The supplies cost the ship ten cents a day per capita.

LIVING IN JAPAN.—Persons who find the climate of our Eastern States annoying and who are seeking for more congenial spots may well consider Hawaii and Japan. The former is warmer but has less excitement and attraction. The south coast of Japan has its season of slight snow falls and demanding fires, but it is never troubled with severe frosts. The lover of skating has been known to shade a small piece of water with mats to keep off the sun and to secure a very thin ice on which to try his skill. This country has also the advantage of many foreign vessels, of telegraphs, of cheap living and of harmless (?) earthquakes. Although many thousands were destroyed a few years ago yet visitors have, it is said, regretted that there was no shock during their stay.

A JAPANESE FAMILY AT MEAL TIME.

Many of the houses are so built as to guard against destruction and it is alleged that no foreigners have ever been killed. Living is very cheap, coal and some necessaries very dear, but what we call luxuries are at very moderate rates.

Then your gold commands nearly two to one in Japanese dollars (called yens).

Many walk with wooden sandals raised several
inches from the ground by two upright narrow
strips running across the soles. These shoes make
a curious noise and enforce a mincing gait.

The hotel waiters move across the floors in socks.

A JAPANESE TAILOR SHOP.

In their little sitting rooms they have a few live
coals to keep their feet warm. It is stated that no
Japanese enters a house wearing the shoes used on
the street. These are always left at the door and
slippers substituted. Obviously the object is cleanli-

3

ness. The men seem so far as legs are concerned to belong to different races. The waiters are about 5 feet high, and their lower limbs are not only very thin, but as if this were a matter of pride they are encased in tightly fitting trousers showing the attenuations to the greatest advantage.

GROUP OF JAPANESE LADIES.

Yet the outsiders are large and the pull-men have muscular calves. I give this name to the jinrikishaw pushers. Cabs are very scarce. In place of them one finds in front of the hotels, the stations and other places, a little gig, large enough for only one person, seat low down and baby shafts in front. It looks like a toy conveyance. It is called a inrikisha. The name means man puller. The traveller must be cautious lest an untimely slip of this new horse should throw the shafts up and pitch the

occupant out backward. Some such accident has
been exhibited by a clever artist whose picture hangs
as a warning at the hotel door. The man who
drags you thus along has no covering below the
knees; is clad in drawers and a loose coat coming to
the hips. His head is covered with a light hat
looking exactly like an inverted wash basin with a
broad brim. His trot is an even jog. In the city
on smooth macadamized streets the work is no
slight affair. In the country where the highways
are narrow and worn occasionally into deep seams
the labor is great, always aggravated when a rain
creates mud. The pay for this hard work is very
small—only 15 cents an hour.

A guide receives two yens ($2) a day and finds
himself. Allowing for the large premium on our
money, the uncertainties of constant employment,
the necessity for a respectable appearance, etc., the
wages seem very small.

The *rikshaw*, as it is generally pronounced, is not
the only peculiarity of the Japanese laborer. He
builds his houses generally with an inside shell (to
guard against the dreaded earthquakes), often without nails; the plane and the saw are drawn towards
the workman; mills are disliked and hand-power is
the favorite.

YOKOHAMA.— This city, although regarded by
many foreigners as the largest in Japan, is really
inferior in population to many of her sisters.   It is

YOKOHAMA—A GLIMPSE OF THE WATER FRONT.

merely the principal treaty port opened to foreigners
in 1859.   It is well situated on a large bay.   Its
harbor is protected by a break-water.   The streets
are well laid out and macadamized.   Some of the
buildings seem to have been constructed without

any fear of earthquakes before the eyes of the owners. Amongst these one notices the Grand Hotel, Domestic Missions and Public Buildings. The picturesque appearance of Yokohama is enhanced by the volcano Fusi-Yama, visible, though at a great distance, in clear weather. Its summit is snow capped and it is said to be 13,000 feet high.

The Grand Hotel well deserves its name. It is two stories high, facing the broad street and the bay, with a splendid garden and fountain in the rear. The large dining room with its mountains of chrysanthemums is a very pleasing sight, and Mr. Louis Eppinger is all that could be desired of a courteous and obliging manager.

DAI-BUTSU.—In the grounds of the "Ko-toku-in" (Jodo Sect) Monastery of Kamakura, situated but a short distance from the village of Hase and the sea-coast, is preserved one of the most remarkable representations of the Buddha which Japan has produced, an image so perfect that it is regarded as the culmination of the art of bronze-casting in that country.

The name, Dai-Butsu, is given to a colossal representation of Buddah. There are many of these images in Japan. A description of one will suffice for all, the differences not being worthy of special note. The nearest to Yokohama is to be found within a short distance of Kamakara. This place

FUSI-YAMA, SEEN FROM KASHAMABARA ON THE INLAND SEA.

is reached by rail and is about fourteen miles (one hour) from Yokohama. The ride is very interesting to the stranger. The scenery is beautifully interspersed with mountains and fertile valleys. The Japanese seem to understand the art of irrigation. They do not dig deep ditches round their fields, leaving the water to find its way to the crops, but they make sure of every drop. The ground is cut into small squares, triangles, etc. The bottom is then scraped to the side and banked up. Thus the land is covered with a quantity of earth basins varying in size from a perch to five acres. The water is then let on to the ground and there it stands, making no trenches, but hundreds of little lakes. Here flourish the rice, the bamboo, and all their crops, in great luxuriance.

The soil needs no plough. The farmer wields an instrument like our adze. But the handle is long and the blade very deep. Struck into the ground it turns up an immense clod.

The houses in the villages are very quaint. They are built like the English cottages with enormous thatching for roofs and sometimes a crop growing on the very crest.

The Dai-Butsu is a mammoth figure sitting on stone. At first constructed of wood, the present bronze image was substituted perhaps six centuries ago. It stood in a spacious temple destroyed about

four hundred years since by an inundation. The
foundations and the Dai-Butsu remain. It represents
Buddah seated, his hands meeting in front. The

THE DAI-BUTSU.

expression of the eyes and face is very pleasing. The
figure is hollow. A small opening at the corner of
the foundation permits an entrance. Inside is a

ladder by which you can ascend to the neck. From
your perch you see a gilded image in the head and
three gilded figures on a shelf. It is reported in the
books that the eyes are of pure gold, etc. But the
sockets appear to be empty.

Murray in his hand-book says:

"The DAI-BUTSU, or GREAT BUDDAH, stands alone
"among Japanese works of art. No other gives such an
"impression of majesty, or so truly symbolizes the central
"idea of Buddhism, the intellectual calm which comes of
"perfected knowledge and the subjugation of all passion."

Mr. Bayard Taylor says in his work "Japan in
Our Day," that "The Monument dedicated to Dai-
Butsu, that is, the Great Buddha, may be considered
as the most complete work of the Japanese genius, in
regard both to art and to the religious sentiment
. . . a gigantic seated divinity of bronze, with
folded hands and head gently inclined in an atti-
tude of contemplative ecstasy. . . . There is an
irresistible charm in the posture of Dai-Butsu, in the
harmony of his bodily proportions, in the noble
simplicity of his drapery, and in the calmness and
serenity of his countenance."

Mr. A. C. Maclay, A. M., L. L. B., in "A Budget
of Letters from Japan," says: "The Dai-Butsu sits
there in the open air, his head looming above the
pine trees, and his face turned toward the peaceful

waters of the ocean, typical of the dreamless Nirvana."

Mr. Percival Lowell says in "The Soul of the Far East," "The Kamakura Buddha, . . . in whose

YOKOHAMA. A GLIMPSE OF THE FOREIGN QUARTER.

face all that is grand and noble lies sleeping, the living representation of Nirvana."

Dr. C. Dresser, Ph. D., F. L. S., etc., in "Japan— Its Architecture," says: " The figure sits in dignified repose with a most placid expression of countenance.

TOKIO—A TRAVELING SHRINE AND ITINERANT CHOIR.

From its forehead protrudes a boss representing a jewel from which light is supposed to flow, and which symbolizes an idea similar to that expressed in our Scriptures, 'I am the Light of the World.'"

The priests in charge of the monastery declare that it is their endeavor to preserve and embellish the Image and Church and to raise a suitable edifice to contain the Dai-Butsu and protect it from the ravages of time and the effects of the weather so they may faithfully hand down and transmit to posterity this relic of mediæval days which they have received from their predecessors as a precious and sacred National trust, and it is therefore hoped that in the interest of Religion, Art and History alike, all visitors will kindly make some contribution to the building fund, as Japan is not a rich country, and to collect a sum of money sufficient to carry out the object successfully is at best a work of many years, especially when it is borne in mind that the Meiji Government has confiscated all ecclesiastical possessions and disestablished the Buddhist church, thereby leaving the priests well-nigh penniless.

There has been a temple in this place since the eighth century, but the image is of much later date. Its precise history is involved in obscurity. Tradition, however, says that the Shogun Yoritomo, when taking part in the dedication of the restored Dai-Butsu at Nara, 1195 A. D., to which place he

A SHINTO TEMPLE, NEAR TOKIO, JAPAN.

had been summoned by the Emperor to supervise
the ceremony, conceived the desire of having a similar object of worship at his own Capital, but died
before he could put his plan into execution. One of
his waiting ladies, Itano, undertook to collect funds
for the purpose, resigned her appointment, and
with the cordial approval of Masago and the Shogun
Yoritsugu, worked with such devotion of heart that
in 1224 A. D., the priest, Joko (who had collected
money far and wide) with the permission of the
Emperor, was enabled to commence the first image
(which was of wood) and it was completed in 1238
A. D. A splendid chapel was also constructed here.
In the autumn of 1243 A. D., the chapel was over-
thrown by a mighty storm and the image seriously
damaged. Again Itano bestirred herself in the work,
being assisted by the Shogun, who provided the
metal to cast a bronze image, and restored the
Temple in all its former splendor.

The image was commenced in the fourth year of
Kencho, the eighth month and the seventeenth day,
and the founder was Ono, an artificer of Yamamura,
in the county of Moda, province of Kadzusa.

This was the first time that such a marvellous
piece of metal work had been thus successfully
attempted in Japan, and the perfect artistic mastery
of form and true beauty and grandeur of outline

which characterizes Ono's master-piece, is a wonderful triumph of Japanese Glyptic Art.

The Temple was completely destroyed by storms twice, once in 1335 A. D., and once in 1369 A. D., but was repaired. Again in 1495 A. D., the buildings were swept away by a tidal wave, but this time the priests were unable to raise funds for their restoration and only the image and the stone foundations of the church were left.

In the period 1711–1715 a Buddhist Archbishop named Yuten rebuilt the priest's residence and a certain Nojima Yasuke furnished money liberally and presented votive bronze lanterns and various ornaments to the church, but the funds failed and the work of complete restoration was abandoned.

THE MEASUREMENTS OF THE DAI-BUTSU ARE:

		Ft.	In.
Height	.	49	7.00
Circumference	.	97	2.20
Length of face	.	8	5.15
Width from ear to ear	.	17	9.20
Round white boss on forehead	.	1	3.47
Length of eye	.	3	11.60
Length of eyebrow	.	4	1.93
" " ear	.	6	6.54
" " nose	.	3	9.22
" " mouth	.	3	2.08
Height of bump of wisdom	.		9.52
Diameter of bump of wisdom	.	2	4.56
Curls (of which there are 830): Height	.		9.52
" " " " " Diameter	.		11.90
Length from knee to knee	.	35	8.40
Circumference of thumb (say)	.	3	0.00

The eyes were pure gold and the silver boss
weighed thirty pounds avoirdupois. The image is
formed of sheets of bronze cast separately, brazed
together and finished off on the outside with the
chisel.

[The following is a copy of an Ode sold at Kamakura by the Priests.]

NATSU-KUSA YA TSUWAMONO DOMO NO YUME NO ATO.[1]

BASHO.

City of dreamland, ruined and sad,
Once home of a people joyous and glad.
All that is left, "a tale that is told,"
Temples dismantled and monuments cold.

Ashes to ashes, dust to dust,
Glory departed, swords turned to rust.
Weeds, all that is left of hearts brave and gay
Who 'erst to the battle went marching away.

Citadel perished, towers fallen away,
Fortress and temple doomed to decay,
Courtier and warrior in panoply bright
Passed like a shadowy dream of the night.

Oh Buddha Eternal! Thus come we and go.

Fleeting is matter, "Sho-gyo-mujo."[2]
Such were thy words, "What waxeth must wane,"
After calm there is storm, after sunshine the rain.
"Naught is a permanence," glory but show

That leads to destruction, "Zesho Meppo."[3]

---

[1] A dream of the past! In place of warriors, the grass and
plants of summer.
[2] All phenomena are evanescent.
[3] They are subject to the law of growth and decay.

TOKIO—A DISTANT VIEW OF THE CITY.

4

OKIO—Formerly YED-
DO, the capital of the
Empire, requires a visit,
although the expendi-
ture of time, muscle and
money finds but little
reward, the usually false
coloring of books and
the cackle of travellers
to the contrary. Those who have plenty of time,
money and curiosity, yet possessing little brains,
make it a vital point to laud everything they
have seen and sometimes that they have not
seen. This in their judgment magnifies their own
importance. Then they encounter a traveller for
rest or for health, who has but a short vacation and
wants simply to see a little in order to break the
ennui of desired repose, they pounce upon him as a
fair victim. He must see *this*, he should on no
account miss *that*, is it possible he has come such a
distance and is to omit the other? To the class of
traveling musquitoes just described, the omission to
visit Tokio would be little short of high treason.
Yet like many enforced routines it does not pay. It
is a very large city, prettily situated on a bay. It
recalls John Randolph's sarcasm on our capital as a
city of magnificent distances. Some describe it as

twenty-four miles in circumference, others say it is
ten miles square. Standing on Atago-yama (a hill)
the town seems to be of huge proportions. The

TOKIO—A VIEW ON THE OUTSKIRTS OF THE CITY.

streets are generally wide. It has a large and busy
population, possesses one line of omnibusses and a
tram road.

The horses are few and very thin. Occasionally you see a large ox pulling a load. The thousands of houses are of frame two stories high. There is a splendid castle, fine government buildings, an Imperial Hotel that well deserves its name, old walls and moat, new walls and moat, two parks, Sheba and Veno (pronounced Wayno), a museum, tomb of Shogun and a number of temples. It may safely be stated that all of these might be omitted by the sight-seer without occasioning a regret. But if a Pagoda is new to him, he will find one here. It is a very interesting structure, not large nor high, yet to an American very attractive. It is red. The large projecting roofs, five in number, are covered with what looks like tiling. Bells hang from each corner. Carvings line each cornice.

A river called the Sumida runs through the city. Here as everywhere in Japan the traveller is attracted by the peace, the good order, the industry, the thrift, the sobriety, the great contentment of the working classes. Beyond all attractions of temples or ruins, the country certainly possesses the great charm of a happy and law-abiding population.

Besides the places described there are other cities in Japan of considerable importance.

Nikko contains the burial place of a Shogun, a

fine mausoleum, a celebrated pagoda and a copper column.

Miyanoshita, famous for its beautiful scenery.

NIKKO.

Nagasaki, one of the finest harbors in the world.

Osaka, the Liverpool of Japan.

Kobe, on the Inland Sea.

IMPORTATIONS OF WORDS BY THE JAPANESE.— The natives of this Empire have been so blessed by Providence that before their European and American experiences they did not use soap, bread or hats.

Their hot springs enabled them to preserve great cleanliness, their plants supplied all they ate and with the exception of some slight head gear worn by the lower classes they went without hats.

Hence they to-day call soap, shavon; bread, pan, and hats, chapeau. Every one has heard that lunch is termed tiffin.

JAPANESE RAILROADS.—Japan can already boast over thirteen different lines of railroads, extending beyond 1000 miles. The speed is not very great. The cars are divided into classes. The difference between the first and second classes is only in the color of the seat covers. The fares are very reasonable and the service good.

The falls of Katsuragawa are regarded by many as very wonderful. The traveller is carried rapidly down a dozen cascades. The boat is staunch. No accidents are reported. When the season favors, three or more feet of water are found in the shallowest places. To preserve the depth, stone walls are built at the sides of some of the descents. The boats are pulled back to the top by men with long ropes, another steering up stream. It takes over four hours

to retrace the passage which occupied only one
hour.

THE INLAND SEA OF JAPAN is one of the few
sights which really pays for the trouble of a visit.

GENERAL VIEW OF KOBE.

It is reached by the steamers plying westward from
Yokohama to Kobe. This voyage takes about twenty-
five hours. The boat stops some time. Kobe stands,
like most of the cities of Japan, on a terraced plain

surrounded by high mountains. In clear weather the view is very picturesque.

From Kobe the steamer proceeds over the Inland Sea to Nagasaki. The voyage takes about twenty-six hours and affords a succession of beautiful views. The sea is sometimes ten or twenty miles in width, then it narrows to two miles, mountains always on both sides. At times a number of islands appear, then a huge castle rock with an arched doorway opens from side to side.

OSWA TEMPLE, NAGASAKI.

It is very suggestive of the Archipelago on the coast of Norway. The bay of Nagasaki and the city make a very pleasing picture. The town has an old temple on a high hill. As is often the case in Japan, you pass under a beam supported some fifty feet from the ground by columns, making an entrance forty feet wide. This however, does not usher you into the temple but simply to a flight of steps leading to another cross-piece with similar supports, and so you pass through a number of portals. At Nagasaki the first was all bronze, the second and third stone.

From Nagasaki a westward course leads on to China and you reach Shanghai, 450 miles, in thirty-six hours.

CHINA.

Latitude of Hong Kong N. 22°.

DIFFERENCE IN CLOCKS.— Noon at Philadelphia, 12.50 A. M. at Hong Kong.

Fares from Yokohama to Calcutta, one ticket, $281. If to Hong Kong, $60; if from Hong Kong to Colombo, $190, but if one ticket from Yokohama to Colombo, $225. The dollars above noted are silver dollars worth in fall of 1894 only fifty cents. The fare in gold is, therefore, one half of the above rates.

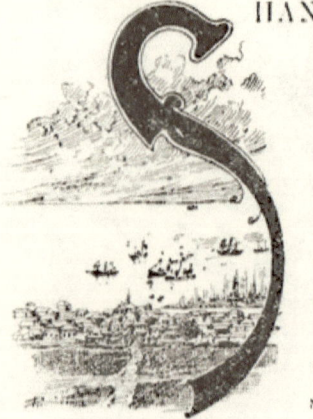

HANGHAI is over fourteen miles up a river. The steamer anchors in the bay, a tug carries the passengers and luggage. The voyage of an hour and a half brings to mind the low flat shores of the Delaware. Some men-of-war are stationed here. The city front is attractive. No miserable, narrow Water street, but a wide avenue called the "Bund" with large stone and brick offices, agencies, etc., greets the stranger with assurance of business enterprise. The city is Chinese only in name. The English, French and Americans have their respective quarters and the British policeman stalks the streets. All the servants at the hotels are Chinamen, receiving about ten cents a day for their kind attention to you. A large import of cotton was at the wharf. One hears of factories which are to inundate the United States with cheap fabrics.

The climate is cold in winter but not very hot in summer. From statements of those who have resided here for years it is quite as objectionable as Philadelphia for a winter residence but the heat of July and August is not so severe as with us.

The Chinese have no jurisdiction over foreigners and all litigation in which the English, French and Americans are concerned is conducted before their own courts.

The marks of English enterprise are exhibited not only in the stately and columned buildings they have erected but in the development of factories.

The Chinese have also been busy. Jessfield, formerly a deserted suburb of Shanghai, is now the scene of a thriving industry. It is termed the Hing Chong Silk Filature. It is situated on the right of the Soochow Creek and covers quite a large area.

A short time ago this was open country. The establishment is the property of a Chinese Company under the direction of Mr. Kienchong and Mr. Maertens. Over eight hundred women and children are employed on 300 reels and basins. When the cocoons are delivered from the interior they are carefully inspected and classified. The large white and even cocoons are ranked as No. 1.

A girl is assigned to every two women. The duty of the child is to immerse the cocoons in boiling

PEKING. THE ENTRANCE TO THE IMPERIAL PALACE.

water and hand them to the women who reel off the silk. The system of charging and accounting is stated to be so perfect that it is almost impossible for any of the property to be secreted.

The machinery is principally of Italian make, the water is supplied by the creek, the lighting is by electricity and the mill is to be run, says the Shanghai paper, night and day, except two months in the year. Ten hours make a day's work.

The enterprise is in able hands and promises well.

The man-puller receives here even less than in Japan. Fifty cents a day for him and his gig is the rate.

On such a wage scale American manufacturers must anticipate a terrible competition, and with free-trade to help the foreign pauper-laborers the American workman may starve. This will perhaps be made more manifest by the study of the report of the British Consul, Mr. Enslie, as to the trade in Osaka for 1893. He says:

"Anyone visiting Osaka now after a lapse of many years cannot fail to be struck with the enormous change which has taken place in the city and suburbs. It was always considered the commercial capital of Japan, but now it may be termed the Manchester of that progressive country. Twenty years ago there was but a single chimney stack in the place, which belonged to the mint, but now shafts rise by hundreds and the air is black with the smoke they emit. Twenty years ago, also, there was but one cotton-spinning mill in the neighborhood of Osaka, situated at Sakai, some nine miles distant and that was of very limited capacity, but at the close of 1893 there were numerous cotton mills in the district with every prospect of a rapid increase, for the Japanese government, with great wisdom and forethought, fosters and encourages industries of all sorts, having the welfare of the people thoroughly at heart."

The rapid spread of the cotton industry in Japan has had a remarkable effect upon the import of raw cotton. Ten years ago, though cotton mills had made a good start, the quantity imported was small, as it only amounted to 2,808,348 pounds, of the value of 247,506 yen for the whole of Japan, whereas in 1893 the import increased to 154,442,368 pounds, of the value of 16,151,570 yen, and of this quantity the Hiogo and Osaka districts absorbed no less than 99,321,825 pounds, or eighty three per cent., being an excess of nearly 19,000,000 pounds on the import of the previous year. On the other hand the advance of the cotton spinning industry had an adverse effect on the foreign yarn trade, for in 1883 the import was 32,854,166 pounds against 25,873,536 pounds in 1893, and it is very certain that the current year will show a still greater falling off in this respect.

Moreover the leading industry of Japan shows an exceptionally good profit to the spinner, and though mills are on the increase their products are steadily increasing in demand so that there is every prospect of the business continuing highly remunerative.

HONG KONG. A VIEW OF THE HARBOR.

A STREET VIEW IN SHANGHAI.

The figures quoted by Mr. Enslie must be a revelation to Manchester. The following estimate is given of producing a bale of No. 20 yarn of left twist, selling in the market at ninety-two yen:

Price of middling Bombay cotton	Yen 54
Cost of spinning . . .	10
Allowance for waste, etc. .	8
Balance (profit) . . .	20
	Yen 92

That this estimate is not at all exaggerated is evidenced by the fact that the leading mills of the district have paid enormous dividends to their shareholders. The Osaka and Temma Cotton Spinning Companies have each paid an annual dividend of ten per cent.; the Amagaski ten and a half per cent.; the Naniwa twelve and a half per cent., and the Hirano and Shenshiu Companies each paid the astonishing dividend of twenty per cent. Mr. Enslie also quotes figures showing the profit accruing during the second half of the year under review to cotton mills for every spindle worked, which in the case of nineteen such establishments selected ranged from yen 1.53 to yen 5.80, and he adds that "much confidence is expressed with regard to still larger profits during the ensuing six months, as the demand is generally in excess of the supply."

The Japan mills are worked upon very sound principles, and in the majority of cases the owners

5

have framed rules and regulations for the comfort and convenience of the vast number of operatives employed which are highly creditable to them, and

LI HUNG CHANG, PRIME MINISTER OF CHINA.

were more especially necessary as most of the mills
worked day and night without intermission. This
state of prosperity has recently received a slight
check owing to the war, and the night work has

A CHINESE PLOUGHMAN.

ceased, but it is hoped that this will only be
temporary.

The trade between China and Japan has long
labored under serious difficulties, and it was not
profitable, because not only was an import duty paid
on the raw cotton but an export duty was levied on

the yarn exported. The attention of the Japanese
government was called to the disabilities under
which the spinners labored, and the export duty
was cancelled, so that a brisk and profitable trade
at once sprang up which was promptly nipped in
the bud by the Chinese authorities when the war
broke out, by the imposition of a prohibitive lekin
tax. It is probable that when peace is established
the Japanese government will take steps to have
this withdrawn, and then no doubt Japan will
supply the Chinese consumer with yarn in large
quantities, which will be in effect an exchange for
the raw cotton they purchase from them.

Contrast the fostering care which the Japanese
Government exercises over this important and
growing industry with the action of the Chinese
authorities. Cotton mills would extend and flourish
in China as much as they do in Japan, did the officials encourage their establishment as they ought
to do, but here the greed of the officials stands in
the way of the welfare of the people, and the industry, which should benefit the millions, is only used
as a monopoly to benefit their rapacious rulers. By
ignorance, obstinacy, cruel oppression and extortion
they crush all enterprise and obstruct the commercial advancement of the nation.

A VIEW OF THE GREAT WALL OF CHINA.

CHINESE AVERSION TO HUNTING.—After foxes had
become an affair of the past in Philadelphia, some
of our horsemen—who ape the English—established
the sport of paper hunting. A member of the party
was sent ahead to distribute small pieces of paper.
After his allowance of time expired the so-called
hounds started in pursuit. They paid no regard to
fences or enclosures, and rode yelling across the
country, regardless of private rights and public
peace. On one occasion—so runs the history—they
came like a thunder-bolt into the newly sown field
of one of our best physicians and noblest of citizens.
He started from his library with his double-barelled
gun, and soon taught the imitators of English lords
that there was a slight difference between a peasant
who should feel honored " you know" by the destruction of his crops, and the gentleman who occupied a
somewhat different position.

See how history repeats itself. Our English
cousins have been trying the fox hunting and the
paper scattering business near Shanghai, but with
something of the same disappointment. The *Graphic*
of October 30, 1894, represents Chinese farmers laying in wait for the hunters, with sickles ready to
wound the ponies. In another cartoon, a bridge of
a single plank is defended by a rough, armed with
a big brush and a bigger bucket of filth. But worst
of all, in a third picture, a dismounted lord loses

his pony and is attacked by an army of Amazons, armed with brooms and shoes. The paper thus describes the sport:

"During the long Shanghai winter, paper-hunting is the most popular sport with riders who do not mind a little rough work across country.

PEKING, A LADY OF QUALITY.

An hour or so before the advertised start of a hunt, the foxes, who are always the winners of the previous chase, accompanied by a few friends, and two or three mafoos (Chinese grooms), set out to lay the paper. This is scattered thickly at short intervals, especially on graves and other raised ground, while one or more checks are given by leaving a gap in the paper or laying a false scent. The distance covered varies from eight to twelve miles, the finish, which is generally a few yards after a good jump, being shown by two flags, between which the hunt must ride.

The object of the hunt is not to catch the foxes, and there are always stewards in charge to start the field and collect it when paper cannot be found, also that after crossing a bridge the foremost riders wait for the rest, and to look after the hunt generally.

The prize for the light and heavy weight winners (the latter having to finish in the first six), is a small cup or an engraved sovereign, and by custom, only winners of hunts are allowed to wear pink.

The ponies for this work are bred in Mongolia, and are sent down in mobs to Shanghai when five or six years old. There the "griffins," as they are technically called, are usually put up to auction, with their rough coats on and untried, and are bought principally with a view to racing, the prices varying from thirty to two hundred taels, the tael, at the present low rate of exchange, being equal to about 2s. 9d. They are all geldings; no mares are allowed to leave Mongolia, as the natives wish to keep the monopoly of the breeding. As a rule they are good weight carriers, and can race carrying eleven stone or more, while twelve stone is a very ordinary weight for them to carry across country. They generally take kindly to jumping, and show a great keenness for sport.

The country is sparsely wooded and extremely flat, the principal raised ground being Chinese graves, which are simply grassy mounds, like the ancient barrows in Europe. There are several of these in each field, and coffins are strewn about " promiscuous," which might have a depressing effect, were it not such an every-day sight. Numerous creeks

PEKING. AN UMBRELLA MENDER.

of all sizes run in every direction, and have to be crossed every few hundred yards by either jumping, wading, or on stone bridges of about three feet in width. There are also numerous dry-cuts, but no hedges and only a very occasional mud wall of two or three feet high. Wheat, cotton, and rice are the principal crops, and nearly every field is cut into ridge and furrow, galloping on smooth grass land being quite unknown.

The natives, it is to be feared, are prejudiced against paper hunters; and, indeed, it is hardly to be wondered at, for, although there is a fund for compensating them for any damage done to crops, etc., as the money has to pass through the hands of Chinese officials it is more than probable that only a very minute portion of the original donation reaches those it was intended for. They show their ill will in various ways, for instance, by digging holes and tying bushes together on the further sides of jumps, gathering up the paper and laying it across impossible places; and woe betide the luckless hunter who comes to grief and whose pony falls in their hands; he may consider himself lucky if he only has to pay through the nose before he gets his mount back. At the finish of most hunts there is a traditional old woman with a hoe, who makes herself generally objectionable until pacified by a silver bribe."

No MAIL SERVICE IN CHINA.—We were told at Shanghai that there was no Chinese mail service. The English have put up street boxes and distribute letters within their jurisdiction. But if you wish to mail to home or to any foreign port the Consul's office must be visited. There is a postal agency where you can buy the stamps of your country and your letters can be dropped into the box in that room.

No civilized conveniences.—There is no underground drainage save for rain. Each person must accommodate himself to the enforced drill of a sick man and take his chances with an earth commode.

Peking.—If a man burn with the desire to see a wretched hole, and is willing to incur the risks of

PEKING. A TYPICAL STREET VIEW.

being stoned, besides enduring fearful hardships, let him penetrate to the Celestial capital.

The best communication now is by boat from

Shanghai to Tientsin. This voyage is made in a steamer arranged for freight, with a small cabin boasting of no state-rooms or comforts. After enjoying this stately trip for two days and three nights, you can reach a railroad, which, if not meanwhile torn up, will carry you fifty miles further. Thence forward for two days more, travelling in palanquin or on horseback, not knowing what will become of your baggage—or your carcass, you may, by the mercy of Providence, reach your destination, with reasonable certainty of not returning during the winter months. Here near the southern gate you will see a fine tower erected on a wall about forty feet high and thirty feet thick, faced with large bricks. The wall embraces a square of sixteen miles, counting all its sides. It has nine gates, of which the front is the largest. All these are shut shortly after sunset. Climbing the wall to enter Peking is punished by death; leaving it in that style is simply banishment. The streets are rectangular, the longest being about four miles. Some of them are very wide, but the residents pile on them their wares, and throw on them all imaginable filth. The carts are heavy. One cannot even indulge in the luxury of a jinrickshaw. These conveyances were introduced sometime since but the conservative Chinese threw them into the ditch.

After a rain the city is a vast mud-puddle. When

DAGOBA IN THE T'IEN-LING-SZ'.
TEMPLE OF CELESTIAL INFLUENCE, LYING WEST OF PEKING.

This monument was erected in the Sui dynasty about 600 A. D., and has many Hindu figures.

the moisture dries the dust is intolerable.   Yet it is
said that the inhabitants owe to this latter annoy-
ance the continuance of their lives as without the
wind and dust the putrefactions would speedily destroy all life.

In this Paradise dwells the " Brother of the Sun,"

A CHINESE FAMILY ON A PLEASURE TRIP.

and here perforce reside foreign legations. The
missionaries are active, and it is to be hoped that
their preaching may tend to the cleanliness which
is next to Godliness.

As the native all over takes to billiards and ten-

HONG-KONG. THE WATER FRONT OF THE FOREIGN SETTLEMENT.

pins, there is hope for his reformation in other matters. It has been suggested that the alacrity with
which the Japanese have become civilized is owing
to their tolertion of alcohol, whereas the Chinese
and Turks abjure it, and remain stagnant. The tea
saloons and opium dens have been so often described
that it is not necessary to notice them.

CREDULITY OF CHINESE.—Although a wary, and in
many cases a shrewd people, the Chinese are, like all
others, more or less liable to imposition. One of them
dissatisfied with the recent defeats, had evidently
received some very curious items of consolation.
When jeered by an exultant Japanese, he quickly
availed himself of his reply. "You no ready for
fight," said the Japanese, "we beatee you bery
quick." The Chinaman waxed hot: "you no
beatee, your Emperor marry sister of de French
kingee, the Frenchee he beatee us."

THE CHINESE ART OF HEALING.—Nothing can be
imagined more satisfactory than the practice of
medicine in China. The patient is offered a number of papers. He selects one. The physician
writes something on it and this is the remedy. The
pharmacœpia is extensive. Every herb is used for
a tea or poultice. But other remedies are invoked.
A piece of the skin of an elephant and the tooth of

HONG-KONG. THE HARBOR WITH ITS AMPHIBIOUS INHABITANTS.

a rhinocerous, powdered and well mixed make a favorite medicine for rheumatism.

FROM SHANGHAI TO HONG KONG is about 800
miles. The voyage is made in fifty-five hours. The
steamer is most of the time in sight of land. The
mountains, islands and fishing boats make a
picturesque scene. Hong Kong is an island about
eleven miles long, and in circumference about
twenty-seven miles. The harbor is surrounded by
mountains and reminds the traveller of Santiago de
Cuba. The city is English. The principal hotel
offices and business buildings are very imposing.

CANTON is distant five hours by steamer from
Hong Kong. It is about two miles in breadth and
six in circumference. It is renowned for its manufactures, jade cutting, lacquer ware, cut glass, silk,
its five storied Pagoda, water clock, the denseness
of its population — estimated at 1,600,000 — the
narrowness and filth of its streets, and the danger
to foreigners. The English occupy a little island
with a moat. At night the bridges are drawn up.
The government undertakes to protect that spot.
Beyond its lines you insure yourself. The thorough-
fares surpass St. Giles. About fifteen feet in width,
a gutter in the center, the pedestrian can touch the
houses on each side. The buildings are very high

and so is the death rate in time of pestilence. I
am told that at such periods 1000 per day is not an
unusual mortality.

MISRULE IN CHINA.—It would perhaps be difficult
to find on earth a people more capable of achieving
greatness than the Chinese. Patient, industrious,
economical, pains-taking, submissive, their empire
could under proper management easily assume its
appropriate place. But it is misgoverned. The
Emperor is a young man about twenty-four years
of age, ambitious to do his whole duty. His mother
and courtiers rule him. He has no time to examine
or correct abuses. He is roused early to go through
religious ceremonials. Then he must receive scores
of officials. He rarely leaves his palace grounds.
When he goes out, four or five times a year, the super-
visors of highways have ample notice, they know
his route, employ thousands of men, the roads are
put in splendid condition, strewn with sand, and
the monarch supposes it is thus always. The mis-
management of the military department surpasses
conception. Shells have been filled with burned
berries, coffee, anything that would resemble
powder. Cannon balls have actually been made of
clay and painted black. Worthless muskets
purchased for the price of old iron have been sold
to the government for ten to twelve dollars each.

A merchant was asked why he did not subscribe to the loan. He said that he kept his wealth where the mandarin could not find it and squeeze him.

THE DECORATED PORTAL IN THE GREAT WALL OF CHINA, NEAR PEKING.

An English gentleman stated that he had been requested to accompany a general on a tour of inspection. The commander of the fort was informed by some runner that his superior was coming. Everything was as usual, dirt and confusion. Men were set instantly at work to polish the cannons. But what was to be done with the accumulations of filth and rubbish. As a happy thought they were crammed into the pieces.

When the inspection was in progress the Chinese official asked the Englishman's opinion. He answered that he would like to examine the inside of the guns. Then came the revelation.

SPEAKING ENGLISH.—Few of them can undertake to talk to a foreigner, others profess to do so but can only utter Iz for Yes.

A gentleman narrates his experience at Hong Kong somewhat in this fashion. He entered a store and asked if the man spoke English. The usual reply was made. The traveller said, Have you so and so?

Chinese—Iz.

Traveller (Looking around)— But you have not got it.

Chinese—Iz.

Traveller—You say you have it?

Chinese—Iz.

Traveller—And then you say you have not got it?

Chinese—Iz.

Traveller—What do you mean? Do you take me for a fool?

Chinese—Iz.

They generally understand, however, sufficient to rule their employers.

They insist upon every member of a family having his or her separate riksha and the same men will not serve two different persons. A lady remarked that she wanted her husband's pull-man to go with her. The answer came promptly, " No, no. you no be my pidgeon." Thus a family of five will require thirty servants.

RELIGION OF CHINA AND JAPAN.—With all that has been written on the subject, it is astonishing that there should be so much ignorance. Some fiercely contend that the two nations are all idolaters, others assert to the contrary. Some will say the Chinese are all Confucians; and then a blank ignorance as to Confucius and his teachings fills up the picture with any back-ground the imagination may supply. The truth is that Confucius never asserted a Divine origin, different in any respect from other mortals. He was born B. C. 551, and was simply a great philosopher. His favorite saying was, " Reading without thought is fruitless, thought without reading is dangerous." Of himself he wrote, "I am an editor, not an author." He never rose to greater dignity than to be Governor of his native province, La. His teaching

was simply an elevated materialism. It served as a
connection between Buddhism and Taoism. These
three religions, now called the San Kiao, are combined in the religion of China to-day. Taoism was

SHANGHAI—A CHINESE TEMPLE.

founded by Li-erl, who preceded Confucius, and was
also his contemporary. He called his system Tan,
"Reason," and taught a future state among the Genii.
Doctor Martin states that the Taoist priests instruct
their believers as to the best localities for building and

for burial and that they only can secure others from
evil spirits. Confucius on the contrary advised " to
keep the gods at a distance," and when he had
finished his " Sacred Books" at the age of seventy,
he returned thanks to Shangti, the "Supreme Ruler,"
for the ability to accomplish this great work. The
five objects of veneration now are Shangti, the earth,
the Emperor, parents and teachers. Shangti is
worshipped only by the Emperor. There are no
idols at his shrine. A simple tablet bears the name
" Supreme Ruler." A bullock is burned and the
Monarch worships before the sacrifice. Had this
remained uncorrupted, the idolatry taught by the
three religions San Kiao would never have adultera-
ted Shangti into the saint-worship of Buddhism or
the degradation of Taoism. Confucius further taught
the most exalted reverence for parents. All that the
child could earn or do belonged to the father.

Nor did the slavery end with life. After the
parent's death there must be lavish obsequies and
ancestral worship. A considerable portion of even
the Emperor's time is devoted to the worship of his
ancestors.

BUDDHISM, as it prevails in Japan, teaches in its
" Diamond Classics," four great truths.

1. That all existence, being sorrow, must be extinguished.

2. That all existence arises from attachment to life or desire.

3. That existence may be extinguished by destroying desire.

4. That this can only be accomplished by Nirvana.

Buddha is a title meaning "The Enlightened." His name was Gautama. He lived some centuries B.C. Doctor Eitel gives the legends which surround Buddha, with the incidents mentioned in the life of Christ ascertained in the Gospels. He is described as born of a Virgin, as transfigured, as descending to Hell, ascending to Heaven, and with every particular in the Saviour's life, save the crucifixion.

Hence the skeptic attacks Christianity as a counterfeit. But alas for the infidel, every particle of this legend is of modern origin. The most ancient chronicles contain no trace of this tissue of invention, and no Buddhist history in existence can take rank in age with the Gospels.

The Veda, the oldest code of Asia, taught the doctrines of metempsychosis and ultimate absorption into Brahma. His priests originated the idea of caste, from their desire to be identified with Deity.

Buddhism intended to reform Brahmanism by abolishing caste, and declared that the means to annihilate self, was "the path to Nirvana." Dr. Eitel states that as long as 2000 years ago, Buddbism "attained to the Darwinian idea of a pre-existing spontaneous tendency to variation as the real cause of the origin of species, but like Darwin and his school, it stopped short of pointing out Him who originated the first commencement of that so-called spontaneous tendency." The student will find this whole subject and many other interesting topics, connected with "The Philosophy of Civilization," most beautifully discussed in a work bearing that title, published in 1889, by Jan Helenus Ferguson, a native of Holland, author of "The Red Cross Alliance at Sea," and of a "Manual of International Law." Mr. Ferguson, after serving his government in various capacities, has, for the last twenty-two years, filled with great credit, the post of Minister Resident to China.

REAL ESTATE SALES in China are made through "middlemen," or agents. After the middleman has arranged the terms of the sale, the grantor executes a deed describing the property, and setting forth the terms of the contract. To this deed the middlemen, of whom there are sometimes several, append their seals as witnesses and as guarantors of title. Deeds are of two kinds, *white* (written on white paper,) and *red* (written on red paper). When real estate is conveyed by *white deed*, the transfer is not recorded in the government books, but remains in the name

of the previous owner. When real estate is conveyed by *red deed*, the sale is recorded, and tax
receipts are thereafter issued in the name of actual
owner. A tax of 3 per cent. is charged on the pur-

HONG-KONG. QUEEN'S ROAD, SHANGHAI BANK AND BEACONSFIELD ARCADE.

chase money (payable by purchaser), for this record.
It is the duty of the recording official to examine
the title, and record is a guarantee thereof. In buy-
ing land it is customary to recieve all deeds inter-
vening between the grantor's deed and the original
owner as recorded in the government book.

Sales are usually made by white deed to save the
government charge of 3 per cent.

Upon death of the owner property is held in
common by the family, and in case of a division, a
larger share is given to the oldest son for maintain-
ing the ancestral worship.

The father has an almost unlimited power over
his family. He can hand the son over to death and
sell the daughter to slavery.

This authority passes in effect to the oldest son on
the death of the father. In a recent case a younger
son could only be relieved from the danger of death
by amputation of the diseased limb. But the older
brother forbade the performance of the operation and
the patient died.

The administration of justice is proverbially cor-
rupt and all the divisions of the government suffer
from this taint. The high officials receive almost
nothing from the State but they make immense in-
comes by selling patronage, promotions, etc. The
Hoppo of Canton (the customs official) receives an
insignificant salary but has, from the other sources,
an income of several millions a year.

The imports and exports in foreign ships or under
foreign flags are in the hands of Sir Robert Hart,
an Englishman. He collects as export and import
duties approximately 5 per cent. ad valorem on all
goods in foreign bottoms or under foreign flags.

This he pays over honestly to the central government. Last year this revenue amounted to 22,000,-

SHANGHAI—A MARKET PLACE.

000 of customs Taels, approximately 22,000,000 of gold dollars.

THE OPIUM DENS have been so often described that like most of the scenes a stranger meets, the picture is worn thread-bare. Every scribbler thinks he can describe better than his predecessor a scene which really requires no description. Why paint anew the listless eyes and dormant forms of a set of opium smokers? Why tell everybody for the thous-

CHINESE MERCHANT AND FAMILY.

andth time that the laborers in these hot holes wear only a girdle round their hips and that the women in some of these places have rings round their ankles?

FROM CHINA TO CALCUTTA.

IN the preceding pages the fares have already been given as far as Colombo. From Colombo to Calcutta the charge for first-class accommodation is 120 rupees— about $30.

The first stopping place of the French steamers westward from Hong Kong is Saigon, 919 miles —sixty-three hours.

Saigon is described as having 14,000 inhabitants, with 80,000 or 100,000 in its surroundings. It is the chief city of Cochin-China and the seat of the Governor-General of Indo-China. It is situated on an arm of the Dong-Nai between two other streams, and has been wonderfully changed within the last few years by France. She has filled the marshes, opened streets and boulevards, built a splendid palace for the Governor, a cathedral, a hospital, schools, an arsenal, stores, a botanical garden, an observatory, etc. The citadel dates from the reign of Gia-Long. It is the work of French officers who were in his employ.

The port is accessible to the largest ships and is furnished with a floating dock. (Condensed translation of Mr. Lanier's excellent work entitled "L'Asie").

The traveller finds himself in a port forty miles

A TAMIL MERCHANT AND HIS FAMILY.

from the sea. The scenery has no striking features, save to an American. The trees are different from his willows, pines, cedars and shrubs. Here are the Banyan with its everlasting roots—reminding one

of the glorious Bacon—who drew from this tree his
magnificent simile of the eternity of the soul. Here
also are the towering palms reaching their heads

SINGAPORE. A GROUP OF MALAY LADIES.

towards Heaven, and all the flora of the tropics.
The heat is at times oppressive—always so in the
sun. But the breeze to-day is cheering and as one
sits at meals the Punka keeps him in an Elysium

7

NATIVE FISHING VILLAGE, JOHORE.

content. This is to us a most curious and a most
acceptable contrivance. Strange that Yankee in-
genuity has never transplanted the Punka, instead
of using the ghastly and ghostly blades of a propel-

SINGAPORE. A MALAY BAND (GAMELANE PLAYERS).

ler to keep off flies and to keep out heat. Here sus-
pended from the ceiling are simple arrangements of
muslin looking for all the world like elongated
bolsters. They are connected by a rope to the side
cord and this pulled by a Coolie sets the whole in
motion and makes you "cooley" indeed.

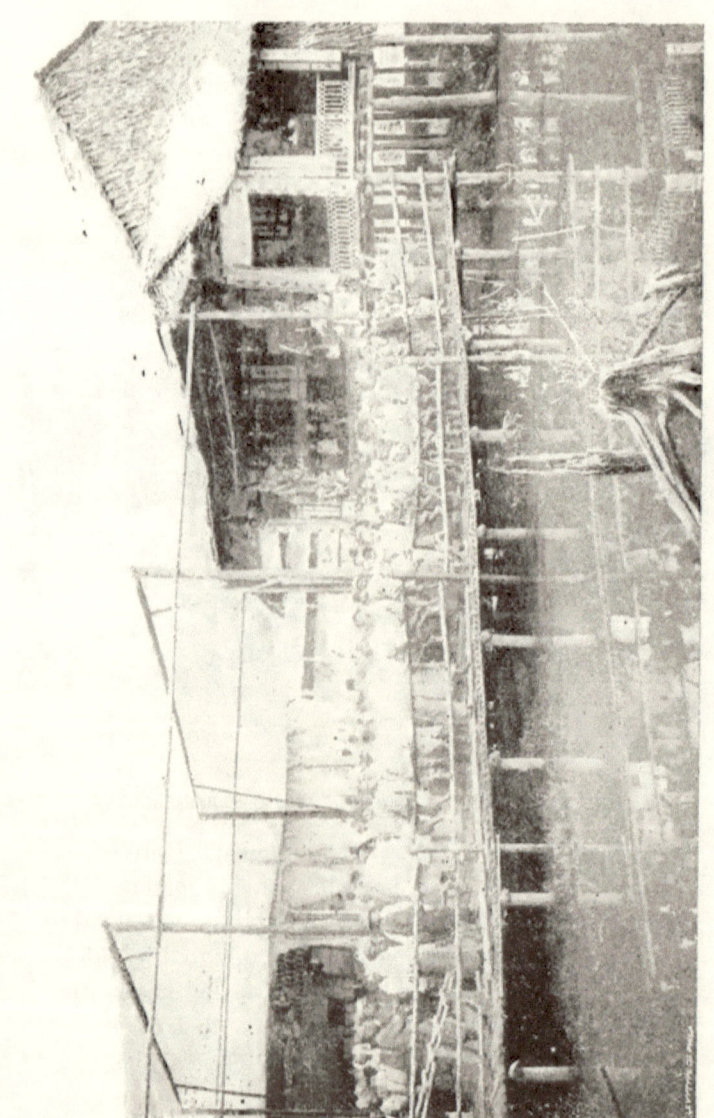

A CHINESE THEATRE AT SINGAPORE.

The clock at this point shows us to be only eight minutes short of the Antipodes of Philadelphia.

The possessions of France in this place exceed by one-sixth her whole Empire in Europe.

GROUP OF OFFICIALS OF THE LAW COURTS, JOHORE.

Saigon is supposed to be malarial. An excursion of a few days leads to a very old temple in Cambodia.

SINGAPORE is distant from Hong Kong about 1550 miles, and from Saigon 637 miles. The voyage from

Saigon is generally less than forty-eight hours. The
town is situated on an island purchased by the
English in 1819 from the Sultan of Johore. Its
population is about 60,000. Within a few miles of

MALAY CHIEF AND HIS FOLLOWING.

the equator the tropical plants of course abound.
The sun like a regular gentleman rises and sets
within a few minutes of six the year round. The
streets are well laid out, and well macadamized.
The public buildings are large and well designed.

The air was balmy—hot—but not oppressive. There is an extensive garden a short distance from the city and within the garden is the nucleus of a zoological exhibition. The traveller is fore-warned to reject here as everywhere the froth and gush of the tourist book. He need not expect to see "tigers and all sorts of vermin." He may be disappointed if he expect to sniff the "spicy breezes of Ceylon." He will find a curious palm, growing straight up some thirty feet with its radii spread exactly like a giant fan. The scenery of the harbor is picturesque. The boys in their light canoes surround the visiting ship and plunge into the water to catch the coins thrown by strangers.

The heat on the steamers is relieved by the punkas kept so agreeably in motion by our friend, John Chinaman.

Colombo (Ceylon) has 128,000 inhabitants. Lanier says the town was badly chosen as the capital of the island; that it is less fertile and more exposed to storms than other locations.

Kandy is in the centre (20,000 inhabitants).

Pont de Galle is to the South (population 52,000) and there are other smaller towns.

The usual running time from Singapore is three days and twelve hours. Arrivals and departures on all these occasions are so arranged as to give the

passengers as little slumber as possible. It is to be
presumed that this produces an economy to the
transporting company. Colombo is the well-known
yet little known capital of Ceylon.

It is not as near to the Equator as Singapore, but
for the practical purposes of furnishing heat in
December to the frozen American and food for the
gush of the book-writer and newspaper man its
latitude of 6° 57′ north is all-sufficient. It is over
5800 miles from London by Brindisi, the shortest
route; and is in time five hours and nineteen
minutes before Greenwich—ten hours and twenty
minutes before Philadelphia. Wherever the English
have improved, one sees fine streets and splendid
buildings. There is not much in Ceylon to justify
a voyage of over 10,000 miles and forty days. But
being detained here for the Indian steamer the time
can be agreeably occupied. You need not take long
journeys to distant points, nor climb fearful ascents
which produce no satisfactory result save the ability
to boast of your prowess and to torture some poor
soul with the degradation of not having come up to
your standard of sight hunting. But you can in all
quietness take rides to a fine park, a parade ground,
the cinnamon gardens, a bridge of boats and a
Buddhist temple.

If your patience permits, you can visit a most un-
inviting bazaar and market. The cinnamon bush

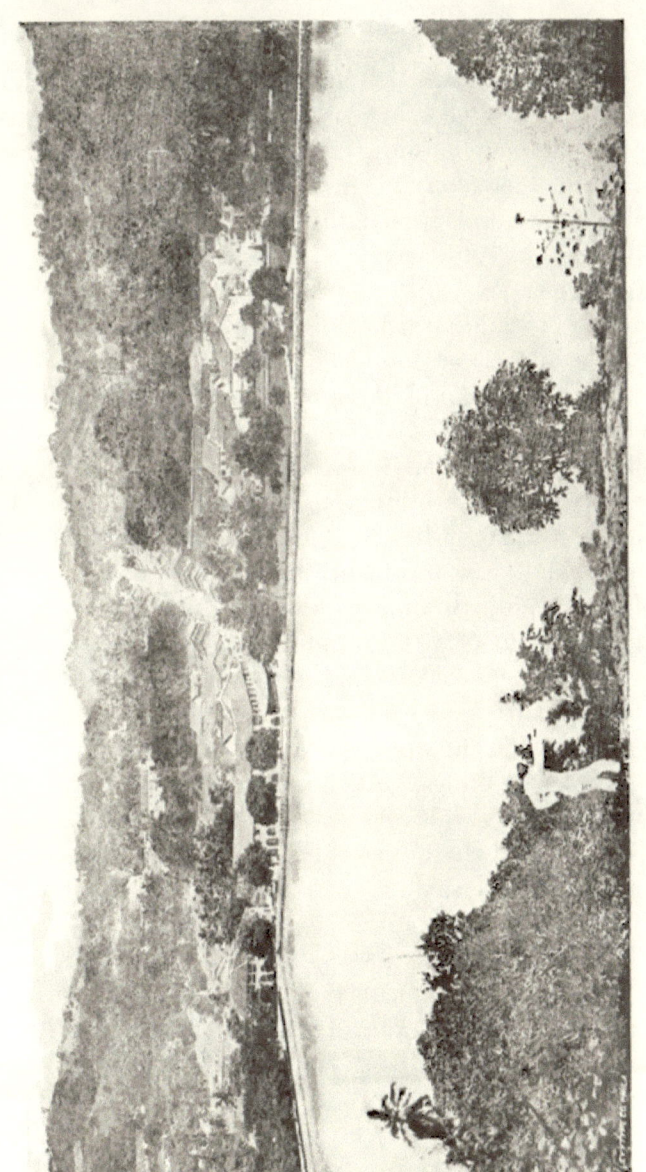

KANDY, FROM ARTHUR'S SEAT.

has no special attraction and save when rubbed the wood emits no odor.

The temple is simply another ugly curiosity. With great ceremony you are shown a reclining figure over twenty feet in length, supposed to represent Buddha. A statue typifies the redeemer, whom his worshippers expect to come. Another figure is the mother of Buddha; at her side is a lotus flower with a little Buddha on top. The sameness, the ugliness and the repetition of these objects make the traveller wonder that he has been stupid enough to get out of his vehicle and pay for being bored. The crowds of men running about with hardly any clothing, some with long hair, most of them with combs, the swarms of children, the panorama all black and swarthy, makes the sight of the ocean and the ozone of its air a most welcome relief.

Colombo enjoyed, during my stay, delightful sea-breezes. Christmas Eve was celebrated at the hotel with a ball. The Episcopal church was beautifully adorned with lillies. All honor to the institution which far over wide seas and distant lands sends its spirit to cheer the hearts of countless thousands and makes even the skeptic say to his neighbor, "Merry Christmas."

THE MAGICIANS OF THE EAST.—The Munchausens have woven such beautiful webs of fiction that it seems cruel, perhaps dangerous, to question them. Not even the cobra of the East can bite with more poisonous fang than the fabulist of travel when you question his accuracy. On one occasion it was my

HINDOO TEMPLE, COLOMBO.

privilege to listen to a trial between two of these truth-destroyers. One gave with great detail the marvels of a diver's skill. He had seen the boy dive from a ship *on the opposite side* when a coin was thrown over and bring it up. His antagonist was not to be beaten by any such paltry feat. *He* told us of a dancing girl in India who bent backwards and lifted a coin from the pavement, not with hands or lips, but with her *eye-lids*. Who has not read of the magician of the East? That supernatural being who can receive without injury the bite of the most venomous reptile, and who can make a plant grow before your eyes from the seed he has planted in your very sight. Now the authors of these stories tell them all as if they were really miracles. No word of doubt or explanation is vouchsafed. How plain a tale will set them down. Whilst you are enjoying a cup of tea at a kiosk your attention may be attracted by a half-naked swarthy native and a boy, who crouch near the threshold. The man carries a small basket about one foot in diameter and four inches deep. He also bears a bag large enough for his conjuring tools. As soon as he catches your eye he pulls from the bag a couple of toys. One of them looks like a short doll, the other resembles a humming top. They squeak when pressed. After a few hideous sounds he takes a pith ball and goes through the threadbare tricks of putting it under a cup; lifting the cup, the ball has gone ; now it is invisible, now it is under the other cup, now it multiplies itself to two, even up to four, is swallowed, thrown in the air, re-appears on some one's nose, etc. Having exhausted the ball game

the basket is opened and out crawls a cobra, as
hideous as deadly.   But it is only a sham.   The
fangs have all been withdrawn. The toy is squeezed
and a humming discord is heard.   The snake lifts
himself angrily, curves one half of his body like an
S and strikes at
the top. He is
encouraged to re-
peat his bites and
sometimes the man
is clearly struck.
But he is uncon-
cerned.   Once the
blood seemed to
c o m e , f o r h e
quickly sucked the
spot and then went
on. After this is
through the snake

BULLOCK CART, COLOMBO.

is seized near the head and a few inches are placed in
the basket.   The reptile is tired of this farce and he
crawls in.   This is really the amusing part of the
play, to see the cobra go back so snugly to his rest.
Another basket is taken out of the bag and the
mango trick is performed.   During the whole of
this the man and boy keep up a sort of perpetual
motion and perpetual squeaking.   The little basket
is opened, a few inches of packed dirt are in the

bottom. The boy inserts a stick some four inches
high, the man throws over it a cloth, and with
many wild words and actions from man and boy
you are informed that something very wonderful
will soon happen. The bag is again resorted to and
a piece of a root about two inches long is exhibited.
This is very carefully packed in the dirt, and the cloth
is restored. The boy always keeps a hand under it
apparently to hold up the stick, but really to per-
form the miracle. More noise; the cloth is withdrawn and a little green leaf appears between the
stick and the dirt, as if it had just budded. Some
one exclaims that this is nothing; that the mango
plant should be created. The Singalee says, "Oh,
yes, but it must have time to grow." All is covered
again, water is plentifully sprinkled under the cloth
and the pow-wowing repeated. At last the muslin
is removed and there sure enough is a mango plant
about three inches above the ground having on it
some eight leaves. It is quickly removed, one leaf
torn off and given to each lady present. It is plain
that the whole affair could have been introduced by
either of the performers, or was more probably con-
cealed in the cloth or beneath the dirt in a false lid
of the basket. The water sprinkled had of course
nothing to do with its growth but was simply to
clean off the dirt.

As represented by Munchausen it is a veritable

miracle, as seen by you it is a mere imposition, not
half as clever as the old ball and cup game. The
concluding scene was to one party at least the most
satisfactory part of the show. The poor snake is
again disquieted. His torturer with the left hand

ELEPHANTS AT FERRY, NEAR KANDY.

seizes the reptile very close to the head and presses
the thumb so tightly on the creature's jaws that I
wondered he survived. Then twirling the cobra
round his neck the Indian with his right hand
carries to each guest the basket lid to gather in his

well-earned rupees, his eyes glittering all the while
not very much unlike the poor snake's.

Fruits, Etc.—It seems strange to find in these
warm countries no grapes, no peaches, no melons

FRUIT SELLERS, COLOMBO.

like those of the United States. Even oranges
seem scarce. The milk is weak; the butter unpal-
atable; the meats tough and poor. The handsome
little buffalo oxen, with their pretty colors, small
horns and curious humps, trot about like horses,
but when worn out they make sad beef. The

STREET SCENE, PETTAH, COLOMBO.

8

viands one sees in the markets leave him no appetite for the table.

The breadfruit tree, the cordaman, pepper bushes and palms, abound. They tell of curious tailor bird

SKINNER'S ROAD, COLOMBO.

nests; but the spicy breezes are all poetry. Bananas and pine-apples are plentiful : salad is rarely served ; tomatoes are scarce.

During Christmas week the banks and nearly all the shops were closed for four days.

CEYLON. PADDY BOATS ON THE RIVER, RATNAPURA.

KANDY.—It is said that this is a favorite shelter from the heat; but Colombo needed no such refuge the Christmas season of 1894; the wind was very pleasant every day and on two nights was quite cool. The houses are all constructed for hot weather; there are no fire places; everything is open doors, latticed, etc. The bedroom I occupied had no window sash, and the outside shutters were arranged with blinds. It seems very strange to a Philadelphian that he should in Christmas week keep carefully out of the sun, wear his thinnest summer garments, lounge all day and sleep at night under a mosquito bar.

Kandy is 76 miles from Colombo, has a Governor's palace and a fine library. Botanical Gardens are near and Delada's Temple was built for Buddha's Tooth.

There is a fine sanitarium at Neura Elliya at an altitude of 2600 feet, 50 miles from Kandy.

These things may be credited, but the *"wild elephants in herds"* and "bamboos that grow one half inch every hour" (2 feet a day—730 feet in a year); we may be pardoned by our friend the story-teller for rejecting.

In place of wandering over the island to gather up fables, let the tourist rest his weary brain and gaze out quietly, as he may by the hour, at this beautiful harbor of Colombo, with its blue sky and

CEYLON. OLD DUTCH CANAL, NEGOMBO.

bluer water, bearing on its calm surface the huge
ships which carry to and from these shores so many
precious cargoes and more precious lives. All this
like a quiet, natural, but lovely picture is spread out

ELEPHANT DRAWING COCOANUTS. BATTICALOA. CEYLON.

directly in front of the Oriental Hotel, and seems to
condemn the spirit that casts one hasty look upon
the scene and turns from it forever.

As our German friends say "so many a student
crosses the Rhine a gosling and comes back a goose."

ADAM'S PEAK is pointed like a loaf of sugar and overlooks all the neighboring mountains. According to the legend, " When Buddha descended upon the earth in a frightful tempest, he rested upon this island, drove out the evil spirits and established his residence here. He proclaimed his gospel Nirvana and taught men to seek happiness by living without desire and by dying without fear. In ascending to Heaven he left not only a handful of hair, but also at the special prayer of the King, the print of his foot. This, called the miraculous sripada, is found at the precise spot where for the last time his foot rested on earth."

It is needless to add that for more than 2000 years pilgrims have flocked to this spot. Eight hundred years ago a temple was erected, and of course a basin was placed there to receive the offerings of the devotees. There is some conflict of statement as to the footprint. The Arabs claim that an angel carried Adam to this peak. The Chinese assert that the mark was made by Iwan-Koo: the Portugese contend for St. Thomas, and a Persian poet has bestowed the honor on Alexander the Great.

The celebrated tooth was in its day the subject of fierce battles. In the 16th century it is said that the Archbishop of Goa reduced it to powder in a mortar in the presence of all the court, and threw the dust to the winds of the sea, yet the faithful insist that the tooth still exists intact.

Mr. Russell narrates the exhibition of it to the Prince of Wales in 1876. The golden box containing the relic, studded with blazing jewels, was placed upon a silver table. A priest opened it. It contained another box. The second being opened disclosed a third, and so on to the fifth, all of jeweled gold. At last the tooth was seen reposing on a lotus leaf of gold. The priest, trembling with emotion, exhibited the tooth to the Prince, who having duly examined it, retired.

From Colombo to Calcutta required a week. The steamer stopped at Pondicherry for a few hours, at Madras for half a day.

Pondicherry is governed by the French. It has broad streets, some fine government buildings and a botanical garden.

Madras boasts of larger buildings and a better garden.

Calcutta is not situated on the coast, but is some eighty miles and odd up the Hooghly River. The navigation is difficult: one cannot go at night and must stop in daytime for the tide. We anchored off the mouth of the river at 2.30 A. M., but did not reach Calcutta until 11 A. M. of the next day, say thirty-three hours.

ACROSS INDIA.

Calcutta, Lat. 22° N.
Time, Philadelphia, 12 noon, Calcutta, 11 P. M.

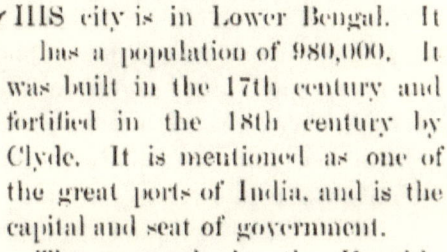

MEWATI DANCING GIRL

THIS city is in Lower Bengal. It has a population of 980,000. It was built in the 17th century and fortified in the 18th century by Clyde. It is mentioned as one of the great ports of India, and is the capital and seat of government.

The approach by the Hooghly River is described by the inhabitants as much worse than it was found during the voyage. In the city we were informed that 2000 years ago the sea swept up to the base of the Himalayas. This word, by the way, is honored with three different pronunciations. The English and the Americans pronounce it with the accent on the *lay*. But the Orientals contend that this is wrong. Some call it Hima-*loy*-yas, others E-ma-loy-as.

After the sea retired the mountains seem to have resolved to return the compliment of an invasion and for years the wash from these hills has brought down avalanches of sand and drift which have been poured into the water and have gradually encroached upon the Bay of Bengal by enlarging the continent. The result has been to make the mouth of the Hooghly a most treacherous entrance. It is constantly on the change. In the open channel of this week there may be poured in seven days a little mountain of sand. Nor is this the worst. Should a vessel strike she can never hope to be relieved by tide or tugs. She begins instantly to sink in the sand. We passed a ship which was buried far down and had sunk so rapidly in the quick debris that only one of her crew escaped.

The climate is represented as very good for four months, including the winter. But in May the rains set in. In summer the thermometer, I was told, rises to 100 degrees and remains there. My informant said that the nights were intolerable. Earthquakes occasionally come, but they seem to be almost harmless. The shakes here are not horizontal; they lift you up and suddenly let you down.

Fort William is a fine structure. The Post office is a grand building. Near it was the famous Black Hole. Then there are the Government House, the Town Hall, the palace of the ex-King of Oudh, St. Paul's Cathedral, other churches, the University, the Indian Museum, etc.

There are also statues of Sir James Outram, Lord Bentinck and others.

The Zoological Gardens boast of some very large tigers and some beautiful birds. The Eden gardens were the gift of two ladies of that name.

Notwithstanding the wealth of the city there seems to be no proper sanitary law in force. The streets are, in the main, good turnpikes, but all matters dropped percolate to some extent before removal and the subsequent sprinkling only seems to perpetuate the disagreeable odor.

The hotels are strangely kept. At our hostelry— very large and grand—a wide marble hall separated bed-rooms from the dining-room. In this beautiful passage were tables used for preparing vegetables, oil stoves and a kitchen.

The tiles were stained very black and the whole had a strange appearance.

Guide books tempt the traveller, as usual, to visit many places he might well pass. First of these coming westward is Benares. It is twenty-seven hours from Calcutta. The sleeping cars are not the subject of extortionate extra charge as with us. It is true that they are not supplied with bedding, nor soap nor towels. The other conveniences are however given.

The first-class car accommodates four, the second class, five persons. There are no chairs. Sofas run along the side of the car and a cushion can be let down making two comfortable beds in each row.

For a few hours a man could rest well enough on
the lounge. But for all night each passenger provides a blanket and a pillow. These cost $1.75 and
remain his property. It is usual to have a male
servant. He carries all luggage, beds, etc. included,
spreads your blanket and makes you comfortable.
His fare and compensation seem almost trifling.
His passage all the way from Calcutta to Bombay
is about $6. The return fare is even less, $4.50.
His wages are only about thirty cents a day, and
out of this he provides his own living. He pleads
for some warm clothing. Two dollars and a half
suffices to supply this, so that a trifle over $20 will
pay for him and the pillow and blankets. When you
put against this our extortion of $5 a night with the
top lid down on you unless you pay $5 more you
conclude that India is more economical.

The first-class ticket from Calcutta to Bombay
covering about 1800 miles is $36.

It is said that there are 2000 temples and shrines
at Benares, and that the city is the oldest in the
world. I see no signs of great antiquity. The few
temples one's stomach permits him to see disgust
him very thoroughly. Gateways, portals, altars, all
the associations of a temple vanish as you approach.
Of course there is an entrance. A few feet off on some
sacred pavement which you must not touch is a doll
seated on the floor, representing nothing human,

tawdrily dressed, hideous and repulsive to the last
degree. You are told that this is a god. Men offer
to it little garlands of flowers and then as a blessing
present the buds to you calling baksheesh. One of

BENARES—VIEW OF TEMPLE AND GHATS ON BANKS OF GANGES.

these hideous holes had gilded spires; they call it
the Golden Temple. Another is the Cow Temple,
still another is the Durga Temple. The attraction
there was to see the monkeys. But even this failed.

I counted three on the roof and two on the ground, ugly and dirty. Yet whilst trying in my humble way to find relief in looking at a poor monkey, two wretches kneeled in front of me, and before I could realize the situation they pulled out of their bags two boas, four cobras and a handful of scorpions which they exhibited for my delectation. Nothing was left save retreat. But this is difficult. An army of men, women and children surround you. Their cries are stunning. Yet out of the din it was sweet to hear in English, " May the good God bless you, sir."

A Rajah's palace, the hospital founded by the Prince of Wales, and some other buildings are pleasant to the eye. But the rest seems to be a rough collection of dirty, squalid houses, unworthy the name of residences.

These are the afflictions brought upon the ignorant traveller by his faith in guide-books.

Up dirty, narrow streets, then turning into a still smaller passage, through noxious odors, you come to a railing about four feet square around a hole. It looks like a well. They burnt some paper, let some embers drop down—down—many feet. Then, they explained that this for years was the spot where the fanatic threw himself to death. As there is nothing of this in the guide book, which contains all the

Munchausen fables, the story is merely stated for the benefit of the next Gulliver.

The Ghats are stone stair-cases leading to the river. You descend some twenty steps, take a chair on a

RESERVOIR AND GARDEN IN THE CHOWMAHLA PALACE, HYDERBAD, DECCAN.

large cranky boat and the men row you a mile or so up and down the Ganges. The view is picturesque. The river bank is over fifty feet high in some places. Every square or so the stone stair-case appears. Sometimes it is in a straight line, again

it curves. On the bank appear temples, houses of
the wealthy, etc. The temples have all the peculiar spire of India. For some forty feet it ascends
in a straight line with four sides; recesses appear in
the work. Then it comes to a point somewhat like
a candle extinguisher. The carvings are quaint.

At the foot of the bank there is a shore way along
the river varying from twenty to fifty feet in width.
This is filled with narrow planks leading to the
water and sometimes you see a small screen. Men,
women and children bathe here promiscuously, save
that there is one place reserved for widows and another for high castes. There are no bathing houses.
The men generally go into the water with an apron
girdle. The women are completely covered with
muslin. They descend into the water but a few
steps. I saw only one man swimming. When
waist deep they dip up the water with their hands,
pray, and gently wash or pat first the forehead and
then other parts. It appears to be a religious bath.
For the cleansing of the body it would seem not to
be very effectual. I have never seen people bathing
in such dirt. A short distance from the shore the
boat passes through hundreds of dirty green subs-
tances floating on the surface. In two places water
descends as from a sewer; and one woman threw in
several baskets of dirt. Here are the cremations;
we saw four piles on fire. The bodies are brought

down tied up in plain material. The red I was told was the female and white the male color. A pile of sticks is built about knee high, the body is placed on the top, then some more wood is placed over it.

CREMATION GHAT AT BENARES.

The whole being about six feet long, four feet deep and four feet wide. Straw is ignited by the principal mourner and thrust under the wood. A son was pointed out as performing this rite. The cre-

9

mation lasts about two hours and then all is thrown
into the sacred River. The chief mourner stays in
seclusion for ten days and then gives a feast. The
scene on the river is full of the curious but destitute
of the cheerful.

LUCKNOW.—The journey from Benares to Lucknow (202 miles) is covered in eight and a half hours.
The land seems to be better tilled and more attractive than it appears near Benares. Cotton, tobacco,
sugar and all cereals are raised in India. With the
exception of the wild cactus and tropical trees the
appearance of the soil is much the same as in other
countries. The railroad and stations are all English.
The residences are almost universally one story
high and according to the rank of the occupants
are squalid huts or stately palaces. Lunch and
dinner are served at stopping places but in rather a
meagre style. The waiters hardly speak a word of
English and the traveler's lot "is not a happy one."

Lucknow is a very handsome city. It is situated
on the river Gomtee, which has the unpleasant
quality of submerging a suburb when it is so pleased.
A tablet marked a terrible rise so recently as September, 1894, and other tablets preserve an unpleasant record. There are many fine drives, splendid
residences, grand mosques and scenes of great historical interest.

Amongst the houses, the Martiniére, as it is called, may probably rank as the largest and oddest in the world. It was erected by General Claude Martin,

GATEWAY OF THE PALACE OF LIGHT, LUCKNOW.

who was born in Lyons, 1735. He served in the French army in India with great distinction, rose from the ranks to high command and was taken prisoner in 1761. He was engaged by the Sawab of Oudh to make some surveys, settled in Lucknow, opened a bank, became immensely rich, built this curious palace and on his death left the bulk of his estate to charities. The building is now used as a school. It has nothing to attract save its enormous size. A critic condemns it as a "fantastic specimen of architecture adorned with minute stuccos and enormous lions, with lamps instead of eyes, etc."

The Sepoys used this place as a fort in the mutiny of 1857. Very different from this are the Mosques. The Immambara (house of the Prophet) in the Muchee Bhawun, the Hosseinabad Immambara, the Jumma Musjid, etc. They are beautiful, white structures, all standing inside of tasty enclosures and of large proportions. The architecture is what we call Moorish. The floors are marble. They all have silver stair-cases inside, of six steps, some leading to a seat whereon we may imagine a monarch sat. They are all studded with beautiful lamps and candle stands six or seven feet high for other lights.

The Mosque first named was built in a time of famine to provide for the starving. It cost £1,000,-000. The length of the centre room is 163 feet, its breadth 53 feet and its height 49 feet. The length of the building is 303 feet, its breadth 163 feet and its height 63 feet. These large proportions are all arranged with perfect harmony.

The Hosseinabad consists of two rectangular enclosures. It was erected by the third King of Oude. The Immambara here is divided lengthwise into three rooms. The central room contains the tombs

LUCKNOW, THE RESIDENCY.

of Mohammed Ali Shah and his mother. The crown and other insignia are exhibited. There is a gilded dome. The floor is paved with black and white marble. In the centre of the square is a model of the famous Taj Mahal of Agra. It contains the tomb of the King's daughter.

Jumna Musjid is the great Mosque of Lucknow. It boasts of lofty and massive pinnacles. Its walls are enriched with arabesques.

Whilst these structures must be accepted as faultless in their way, there is yet a sameness about them. Who sees one sees all. Of far more interest to the Anglo-Saxon are the scenes here which are full of historical interest.

Chiefest of these is the *Residency*. It is now in ruins. It was built by a Nawab about the year 1800 for the British Resident at his court. It is one of the higher spots in the city. There are several large buildings near to it. One a dining room, another a doctor's house. There seems to be a cluster of buildings. The reader knows of the mutiny which broke out at Lucknow May 30, 1857. The Residency was besieged from June 30 to September 25. Cannonades, minings, assaults were all resorted to with overwhelming odds in favor of the mutineers. Every attack was repulsed, but the buildings threatened to fall. The walls are honeycombed with the marks of the shells. When at last Havelock and succor came the brave forces of 1692 had been reduced to 979. General Neill fell during the action on the last morning.

As usual in those cities there are the old quarters

THE GREAT MOSQUE OF NURENGZEBE ON THE BANKS OF THE GANGES AT BENARES.

and the bazaars. They are all alike. A passage
hardly wide enough for one vehicle and the crowd
of pedestrians, is lined with two story buildings—
some frame, some mud and some plastered. These
are thronged with hard-working artizans and patient
sellers. At one spot a score of shoemakers, further
on workers in brass and other metals, embroiderers
of cloth, silk, muslin and a multitude of avocations.
The workshop, factory and shop may be one room,
no bigger than a large kennel, say eight by eight.
Here are sometimes two men hard at work. Several sewing machines were seen. Behind is a room
of the same size where the family reside. Would
free trade introduce to the United States this life for
the American workman?

To the credit of Lucknow it should be recorded
that her bazaars were clean and orderly. No foul
odors here salute the visitor. The climate in this
section is very pleasant for half the year, but the
rains bring intolerable heat and the snakes come
out to get dry.

A traveling companion seems in dread of hostile
visitations even now. He examines his room before retiring and puts his shoes on a chair to avoid
making the acquaintance of a scorpion in the morning. Caution is a useful friend but fear is a cruel
tyrant.

This hotel (The Imperial) is very large and is well

kept. There are no second stories. The centre
building and its long wings have wide arched corridors in front, all fireproof. The bedrooms are of
good size. In the rear is a bathroom. It is supplied with toilet table and washstand. There is no
bathtub, no water closet. In place of the latter is
the old fashioned commode. The bath is a curious
arrangement. A space about six feet square is plastered and around it is built a little wall about ankle
deep. Within are four earthen jars full of water
and a large bathing pan. On the level of the floor
is a little hole out of which the water runs. Back
doors admit the servant who comes unbidden.

CAWNPORE.—Two hours on the rail take you from
Lucknow to Cawnpore. Around this town will
cluster for all ages the sentiment which commands
sympathy for suffering and indignation against
cruelty. The events which make it memorable
have been too often written and are too well
known to need repetition. Whilst the greater part
of the soldiers were at church, their principal building was seized by the mutineers. A miserable entrenchment was held by General Wheeler and his
heroes for twenty-one days, against a continuous fire.
The well, from whence the water needed by the besieged was to be drawn, stood outside the entrenchment, and the supply was only to be secured at im-

minent peril of life. The presence of a number of
women and children in the English camp doubtless
induced the General to listen to an offer to transport
all in safety, if the place were surrendered. Boats
were provided and the whole camp was marched to
the Suttee Chowra Ghat, a landing place on the
Ganges about a mile from the entrenchment. Nana
had arranged his plans with minuteness of atrocious
detail. The boats were all roofed with straw, some
men were detailed to set fire to the boats on the
raising of a flag, others were ambushed on the banks
to rake the barges with their guns, and as if this
was not enough, cavalry was detailed down the shore
to cut off any who might escape. At the given
signal the matches were applied, the fusilade commenced and all were slaughtered save two soldiers,
Thompson and Murphy, and a band of women and
children, who were hurried to the town and confined
until the approach of succor when they were bar-
barously murdered and many thrown down the well.
The traveller sees the well, the lines of the old camp,
and the bullet marks at the wharf. The names of
the unfortunates are preserved on tombs and on
brass tablets in the beautiful church. In the Park
there is a glorious figure of an angel in marble. It
was designed by Baron Marochetti, and is surrounded
by a chaste gothic screen. At the foot of this mound
are the tombs of many who fell in the mutiny.

JAMDER RHAMAN PALACE AND GARDEN, GWALIOR, INDIA

The Ghat referred to as the place of embarkation was a brown building where Hindoo women disrobed before bathing in the Ganges. Along the river banks are still marked the spots where the unfortunate widows went through the rite of Suttee upon the funeral piles of their husbands. If England and Christianity had done nothing more for humanity than the abolition of this horrid rite—the enemies of both should rise up and proclaim their greatness.

AGRA is one of the most attractive cities in India. It is nearly six hours by rail from Cawnpore. The streets are generally very wide and well turnpiked. The bazaar has a broader thoroughfare and is more inviting than the rival cities. Many of the houses in the narrow quarter have second stories, with marble verandas. The city is on the right bank of the Jumna. On approaching it attention is attracted by the large Fort. Its walls are seventy feet high, with a circuit of a mile and a half. It is built of red sandstone, has huge towers and presents an imposing appearance. There is a drawbridge, a deep, wide moat, a huge gateway, and a long, curved ascent which strikes the mind as a pretty serious obstacle to an assaulting party. After reaching the top of this hill and passing an inner portal, you are in the palace buildings. These monarchs must have enjoyed the pleasures of this life. A lake, it was said, was in one of the squares. It is now filled up. Here, in excellent preservation, are a hall of public audience, a hall of private audience, each with its throne, a court 500 feet by 350, surrounded by arcades, many corridors, the Queen's bed and bathrooms, etc. All of these are of white marble and are beautifully carved. It is said that here 500 people were lodged. From one of the battlements could be seen in a court yard frequent exhibitions of wild beasts. The Harem, the grated windows, the private apartments of the illustrious Arjumand are all pointed out. Here too, alas, is shown the place where Shah Jahan, who had ruled over all this with so much glory, was confined after being dethroned by his son.

The oldest parts of the structure date from the reign of Akbar. The inscription over the main archway of the Jumma Masjid (Great Mosque) shows that it was built by Shah Jahan, commenced in 1639 and finished in 1644. During this period he was also engaged upon the tomb of his wife. He was deposed by Aurangzeb, who built the public audience hall above mentioned in 1685.

This large pile embraced a small city, a palace and a fort. Though possessing no strength as against modern artillery it must have been originally regarded as a mighty stronghold—the seat and the witness of great power.

THE TAJ MAHAL is a beautiful white marble
tomb erected by Shah-Jahan in honor of his wife
Armajund. The carvings are very chaste and the
entire pile does credit to the virtues of the wife and
the love of the husband. It was commenced shortly
after the death of the Queen, 1629, but was not
finished until 1648. It has been so rapturously
described by scribblers that it seems difficult to present it in its true colors. It is not "a dream." It
does not "baffle description." It is in appearance
exactly like a mosque. Not so large as the largest,
nor by any means a small building. Like the tomb
of Akbar and other illustrious persons, it is not pro-
truded upon a highway. You enter a gateway
which is itself a handsome and large building. You
drive a few hundred feet, then on foot enter another
imposing gateway structure and find yourself 700
feet from the Taj. These distances are not from
measurements save by the eye. The grounds stretch
out as if you were in a Park. In front is a broad
stone walk divided by a shallow sheet of water with
ends of pipes at regular distances, as if for fountains.
On both sides are flowers. The walk half way is
broken by an ascent of a few marble steps and you
are at the side of a large basin of water. Passing this
you descend again and thus you approach the tomb.
Its size may be understood when you imagine a
building of excellent proportions whose dome is

eighty feet above the roof. The crescent was estimated by a gentleman at my side to be 180 feet from the ground. A writer calls it 243 feet high. The mausoleum is in depth and width 186 feet. Inside is a large octagonal room. Two tombs—one of the Emperor, the other of his wife, are shown on the floor. But they are not the tombs. On leaving you are invited to descend to the basement and there indeed are the resting places of the loving husband and the faithful wife. Many panels are inlaid with agates and colored marbles, but white is the prevailing color. The main building stands on a plateau; at each corner is a marble tower, and a minaret, 137 feet high. There is a mosque on each side. A florid writer states that this structure cost £2,000,-000, and that 20,000 men were employed on it for twenty-two years. He adds that "while gazing on the Taj men let their cigars go out and ladies drop their fans without noticing the loss." Let all men reading these statements draw the veil of charity over the delusions of the gusher.

It is related of Armajund that a slave was brought before her who had attempted to alienate the love of the Emperor. The Empress drew a dagger as if to slay her rival, but then inserting the point in the ground and breaking off the blade, she bade the offender to note the vengeance of a Queen.

The Pearl Mosque is near to the Fort. It has

three domes of marble with gilded spires. It was
built by Shah-Jahan in 1654. There are no pearls
in it and a traveller near me who asked "where the
pearls were" seemed disappointed.

The tombs of Akbar, of Itimad-ud Dowlah and
many other places are worthy of a visit simply to
while away time; but would not justify much labor
or expense for their inspection.

JAMMAH MASJID DELHI

DELHI is six hours by rail from Agra.
It strikes the visitor as a more
thriving and imposing city than
Agra. Approaching towards the
west appearances improve. Shah-
Jahan ruled from 1637 to 1658.
He commenced this place in 1648.
Ten years later the Palace Fort
was constructed. It has a circuit
of one mile and a half. The walls
of the city extend five miles and a
half. The principal entrance to
the Fort is by the Lahore Gate.
It has a strong resemblance to the
citadel at Agra. High walls of red turrets, battlements, moat, double portals, etc. The Palace
contains beauties of marble and of gilding one
does not find elsewhere. There is a vaulted hall,
375 feet long, which has been pronounced "the

FORT AGRA.

noblest entrance to any existing place." There are
the large basins for fountains, the Private Audience
Hall, the apartments for females, their bathing
rooms, the King's bed room, his bath room, etc. All
these are of white marble, most of them beautifully
carved with fine traceries of vines, flowers, etc. The
Private Audience Hall is open on all sides, the roof
being supported by square columns beautifully inlaid. In the centre formerly stood the famous Peacock throne. Nothing now remains of it, save the
marble steps and platform. It is described as having been a chair of solid gold five feet long, four
feet broad, backed with precious stones, arranged
like a peacock's tail, glittering with rubies, sapphires
and diamonds. Some report the ceiling as silver,
others say it was of gold. It is estimated to have
been worth $30,000,000, far too valuable to endure.
All this has been carried off by the spoiler. The
large marble stone in the centre of the King's bath
was used for shampooing or massaging the royal
body. The baths are all beneath the level of the
room, about five feet deep, and six to eight feet
square; the supply and exit passages are still here.
On the corner panels of the Audience Hall is in-
scribed in Persian, "If there be a Paradise on earth,
it is this, it is this," reminding one of Moore's celebrated eulogy on Cashmere

" For if this world discloses
Delights unknown elsewhere,
'Tis at the Feast of Roses
Within thy Vale Cashmere."

There is a very beautiful Pearl Mosque near the Fort, and one of the largest mosques in India, perhaps in the world is within a short distance. It is the Jumma Masjid. It stands on an eminence and is reached by a number of steps. These are studded with beggars—men, women, children—many of them sellers of pigeons. The court is 450 feet square, and it is said that it will contain 50,000 worshipers. The arched ways at one end are covered and the ceilings are beautifully carved. Three domes of white marble and two minarets at the front adorn the roof. A little house at the end of one of the long corridors has gilded doors. These are opened and the attendant reverently entering, shows you in succession sheets of the Koran written by Mahomet's son-in-law, a bound volume containing similar copies all in Arabic, a slipper of Mahomet, his footprint on a stone resembling agate, and lastly in a phial, about three inches long, a hair of the prophet. This is one single hair, slightly auburn.

KOOTUB MINAR is about eleven miles from Delhi. The road takes you past ruins of several cities, forts, many tombs, mosques, etc. During the whole ride

something dilapidated is always in sight, at times
you can count half a dozen domes, all going to decay. The Emperor Humayon's tomb is less than
half way to Kootub Minar. It was built by his
widow and it is pleasant to note that at Delhi and
at Agra the memories of a deceased wife and a departed husband have been touchingly appreciated
by the survivor. This structure is in the middle of
a platform and it is over 100 feet square. The platform is ornamented with arches and has four flights
of steps. The mausoleum is of red stone inlaid
with marble. The floor is of the same material
and as usual there is a marble dome. There is a
variety, but at the same time a uniformity in these
buildings. They soon become tiresome except to
the enthusiast.

The Kootub Minar is also spelled Kutab Minar.
It is a curious column. Its outside is grooved and
it looks like an enormous Japanese umbrella closed.
It is reported as 238 feet high, 47 feet diameter at
the base, upper diameter 9 feet. Fergusson reports
the Kutab and its surroundings as "by far the most
interesting group of ruins in India, or perhaps in
any part of the world." The qualification of the
latter part of the compliment is very proper. It is
reported as dating from 1200 to 1220. It is situated
near the centre of a large square. Behind it are ruins
of three arches, the centre about thirty feet in height.

At the side on a slight elevation are four more arches, the centre being about the same height as the first series. The walls of these entrances are nearly nine feet thick. Around the sides are corri-

TOMB OF THE EMPEROR HUMAYON, DELHI.

dors and in front of the arches is an iron pillar about twenty-two feet high. The lowest diameter is sixteen feet. It was erected by Rajah Dhava and its history is recorded in cut Sanskrit A. D. 319. We were told all these details and that the square

referred to was called Butkliana. No great depend-
ence is to be placed upon guides. But if this infor-
mation be correct, then according to Fergusson
these pillars "are among the few examples to be
found in India that seem to be overloaded with
ornament, there not being one inch of plain surface
from the capital to the base: still the ornament is
so sharp and so beautifully executed, and the effect
in their present state of decay and ruin so picturesque that it is very difficult to find fault with what
is so beautiful." The same remark may be applied
to the arches and to columns in the rear. A gentleman called my attention to the fact that many of
the carvings represented ropes and bells.

I said that the Kutab resembled in its flutings a
huge umbrella closed but uncovered. The shaft
has twenty-four indentations or projections, as one
may please to call them, on its face. These are
caused by twelve curves, and twelve angles, all projecting outwards. The prevailing color is red chocolate. There are four balconies or stories. From
the ground to the first overhanging balcony there
are five upright rows of columns carved at top and
bottom several feet deep. It is said that the inside
steps number 379. To walk around the base required eighty-six paces.

I was told before I went there that it was the
most wonderful sight in the world, and that before

the erection of the Eiffel tower it was the highest structure known. Is it a pity that the imagination of some persons is so very elastic? or is it best that they should enjoy these beliefs?

KOOTUB MINAR, DELHI.

On the return journey one sees an observatory and a large equatorial amongst the hundreds of ruins. Some idea of the importance of Delhi may be gathered from the following list of these structures:

RUINS AT DELHI IN CHRONOLOGICAL ORDER.

Name of Building or group of Buildings.	Probable Dates.	Name of Sovereigns.
Adam Khan's Tomb	A. D. 1562	Akbar the Great.
Akbar the II., Tomb of		
Ala-ud Din's Gateway	A. D. 1310	Emperor Ala-ud Din.
Ala-ud Din's Palace	A. D. 1295–1317	Emperor Ala-ud Din.
Ala-ud Din's Minar	A. D. 1311	Emperor Ala-ud Din.
Arab-ki-Sarai	A. D. 1556	Emperor Humayou.
Asad Burj	A. D. 1658	Emperor Shah Jehan.
Asoka's Pillar	B. C. 300	By King Asoka.
Azim Khan; also called Taga Khan, Tomb of	A. D. 1562	Akbar the Great.
Balban's Tomb	A. D. 1330	Built by Nizam-ud-Din.
Baoli or Well	A. D. 1605–1626	Emperor Jehangir.
Bara Pul	A. D. 1523	Emperor Toghlak Shah.
Barber's House	A. D. 1351–1387	Firoz Shah.
Begampuri Fort and Masjid	A. D. 1488	Sultan Behol Lodi.
Behol Lodi, Tomb of	A. D. 1526	Emperor Firoz Shah.
Buddi Manzilla or Burj Mundal		
Bath Khana, the only relics of Hindu period	Hindu Period	
Cashmere Gate		
Chandni Chawk		

CHRONOLOGICAL LIST—Continued.

Name of Building or group of Buildings.	Probable Dates.	Name of Sovereigns.
Chausat Khamba	A. D. 1600	Akbar the Great.
Clock Tower		
Dargah of Yusaf Kutal	A. D. 1488-1516	Sikandar Lodi.
Delhi Fort, modern	A. D. 1658	Emperor Shah Jehan.
Delhi Institute		
Delhi Roshan Chiragh	A. D. 1351	Sultan Behol Lodi.
Delhi Sher Shah	A. D. 1540-1545	Sher Shah.
Diwan Am	A. D. 1658	Emperor Shah Jehan.
Diwan Khas	A. D. 1658	Emperor Shah Jehan.
Diving wells near Mahrauli		
Elephant Statue, the.	A. D. 1565	Akbar the Great.
Fatahpuri Masjid	A. D. 1640	Emperor Shah Jehan.
Fazalullah or Jellal Kabu, Masjid of	A. D. 1528	Emperor Baber.
Firozabad	A. D. 1351-1385	Emperor Firoz Shah.
Firoz Shah's Lat	B. C. 250	Emperor Firoz Shah.
Fort and Palaces of the Mughals	A. D. 1658	Emperor Shah Jehan.
Fort Lal Kot	A. D. 1060	Built by Anang Pal II.
Fort of Salimgarh, the	A. D. 1546	Selim Shah.
Fort of Rai Pithora or Khas Kilah	Hindu Period	Built by the Hindu Ra-
Firoz Shah's Kotila	A. D. 1351	Built by the Hindu Rajas

CHRONOLOGICAL LIST.—Continued.

Name of Building or group of Buildings.	Probable Dates.	Name of Sovereigns.
Great Mosque of Kutab-ul-Islam	A. D. 1191–1250	Katab-ud-Din.
Group of four Tombs facing Safdar Jang's Tomb	A. D. 1370	
Hauz Khas	A. D. 1380	Firoz Shah.
Hazar Seitun	A. D. 1328	Fagar-ud-Din.
Haji Baba Rose Bedi's Tomb	A. D. 1195	Shahal-ud-Din.
Humayun's Tomb	A. D. 1551	Akbar the Great.
Imam Zaman's Tomb	A. D. 1535	Humayun.
Indraprastha or Purana Kila	A. D. 1555	Raja Dhava.
Iron Pillar, the famous	A. D. 319	Sher Shah.
Isa Khan, the Mosque of	A. D. 1540–45	
Jahanara, the Tomb of Princess	A. D. 1680	Aurangzeb.
Jehangir, the Tomb of Mirza	A. D. 1832	Akbar II.
Jaina Temple in the City		
Jamali Kamali, the Tomb of Maulvi	A. D. 1535	Emperor Humayon.
Jama Masjid	A. D. 1629–1658	Shah Jehan.
Jantar Khaina Mosque	A. D. 1354	Firoz Shah.
Janter Manter	A. D. 1720	Mahmud Shah.
Joge Maya, The Temple of	Hindu	Hindu period.

CHRONOLOGICAL LIST—Continued

Name of Building or group of Buildings.	Probable Date.	Name of Sovereigns.
Kadam Sharif		
Kala Mashal, Mosque	A. D. 1652	Shah Jehan.
Kalan Masjid	A. D. 1351–1385	Firoz Shah.
Kalka Devee's Temple	Hindu	Hindu Period.
Khan Khana, The Tomb of	A. D. 1636	Emperor Akbar.
Khirki, Fort and Masjid	A. D. 1385	Emperor Firoz Shah.
Khusrau, The Tomb of Poet	A. D. 1350	Tughlak Shah.
Kilah Kona Mosque	A. D. 1540	Emperor Humayun.
King's Bath		
Kutab Minar	A. D. 1200–1220	Kutab-ud-Din.
Kutab-ul-Islam, The Great Mosque of	A. D. 1191–1220	Kutab-ud-Din.
Lal Bangalow	A. D. 1500	Emperor Humayun.
Lal CHAUK	A. D. 1721	Built by Akbar's Nurse.
Lal Darwaza, Gateway of the Palace of Firozabad	A. D. 1540	Sher Shah.
Lal Kote, a part of the Fort of Rai Pithora	A. D. 1060	Hindu Period.
Lila Burj, Tomb	A. D. 1596	Pathan Sovereigns.
Mahammad Shah, The Tomb of Emperor	A. D. 1739	Mahammad Shah.
Metcalfe House or Tomb of Mohammed Koli Khan	A. D. 1655	Akbar the Great.
Mobarakpur Kotla	A. D. 1540–1545	Sher Shah.

CHRONOLOGICAL LIST — Continued.

Name of Building or group of Buildings.	Probable Dates.	Name of Sovereigns.
Moti Masjid . .	A. D. 1640	Aurangzebe.
Nakar Khana or Music Gallery .	A. D. 1632 . . .	Emperor Shah Jehan.
Nizam ud-Din's Tomb, The Aulia .	A. D. 1321 . . .	Tughlak Shah.
Purana Kilah, Kilah Kona also called Indrapat	Repaired in A. D. 1535	By Humayun.
Queen's Garden . .		
Rang Mahal	A. D. 1635.. .	Emperor Shah Jehan.
Roshan Chiragh, Delhi	A. D. 1351–1385 .	Sultan Betol Lodi.
Rohan-ud-Daulah's Mosque, or Somerhi Masjid	A. D. 1721 . .	Mahammad Shah.
Royal Tombs in Mahrauli . . .		
Rukan-ud-Din, Firoz Shah . . .	A. D. 1250 . .	
Safdar Jang's Mausoleum . . .	A. D. 1753 . .	Ahmad Shah.
Salimgarh	A. D. 1546 . .	Salim Shah.
Sekander Lodi, Tomb of . . .	A. D. 1455 . .	Lody Family.
Shams-ud-Din Altamasha, Tomb of	A. D. 1235 . .	Sultan Rukan-ud-Din
Sher Dandal	A. D. 1556 . .	Humayun. [Firoz Shah.
Sultan Chauri, The Mausoleum of .	A. D. 1211–1236 .	Sultan Gori.

CHRONOLOGICAL LIST—(Concluded.)

Name of Building or groups of Buildings.	Probable Dates.	Name of Sovereigns.
Sat-pula-Bund	A. D. 1380	Mahommed A'dil.
Syad Abid, Tomb of . .		Tughlak Shah.
Taga Khan's Tombs	A. D. 1562 . .	Akbar the Great.
Tir Burja, viz.: Bara Khan, Chhota Khan, and Kali Khan . . .	Date unknown . . .	Of the Pathan Period. [Shah.
Tughlakabad	A. D. 1325 . .	Ghazi-ud-Din Tughlak [Shah.
Tughlak Shah, The Tomb of Emperor .	A. D. 1305-1325 .	Ghazi-ud-Din Tughlak
Unfinished Minar	A. D. 1311	Ala-ud-Din Mahammad [Shah Khilji.
Zinát-ul-Masjid	A. D. 1710 . .	

EYPORE is over ten hours by rail from Delhi. The wayside lunch and dinner are better than at some places farther East. But the wretched hurry, ringing of bells, etc., destroy all comfort.

Jeypore is the seat of a Maharajah. We were told that Maha meant great, so that a Maharajah is superior in rank to a rajah.

Thirty-eight different castes in this blessed country look down each upon the other with supreme contempt. Effigies of all are exhibited in the museum here. The waxen figures present striking contrasts. Two of them strangely enough have shirt collars. Their brethren must regard them with peculiar horror. This city has much finer buildings and more of them than Benares, Lucknow, Cawnpore, Agra or Delhi.

The wide streets are lined with houses two and three stories high, painted a pretty pink or chocolate, traced with white arabesques. Thousands of pigeons and some monkeys are seen enjoying their freedom. The Hindu to his credit be it said, respects the birds. There is a fine park with the usual specimens of trees, flowers, peacocks and other birds, etc. The tigers have a separate establish-

JEYPORE. PROCESSION AT A FAIR.

ment at a distance. When news reaches the Maharajah of a tiger being seen near a settlement his men are sent out and the animal is captured. Sometimes a net is spread across a path into which he is driven. Sometimes a pit is dug, straw and a goat placed on the top. When snared the animal is starved until very weak; he is then chained and placed in his cage; occasionally a cub is caught and we were told marvelous accounts of the little fellows being raised to tameness and maturity, walking about like cats, suffering children to tease them, etc. However this may be, it is certain that the leopard is tamed so as to assist his master in catching antelopes. It is quite comical to see the beast seated upright by the side of his keeper, directly on the highway. The tigers here are fine specimens, but not as large as those at Calcutta.

The factories where baser metals are inlaid with gold, where polished tiles are made, fine work done on metals, cloths, clay, etc., are all worthy of visits.

The most skilled workman receives but one rupee (about twenty-five cents) a day.

The palace is a fine building. You pass through several gates and then through two court yards containing residences for hundreds of eunuchs and others before you emerge upon the main edifice. It is very high and surmounted with the usual ornaments. At the side are a large audience hall and

GIRL'S SCHOOL AT JEYPORE.

an extensive banqueting room.   In the rear are
beautiful gardens with numerous fixtures for fountains, illuminations, etc.   It is said that these cost
a very large sum, but there is a sameness about it
all suggestive of other places. Chatsworth differs
from Kew, and both from Hyde Park. Versailles,
Berlin, Vienna, Madrid, Boston, New York, Philadelphia, each has a distinct type. But here with
very slight variations all are alike. White marble
abounds, but is rarely allowed to stand upon its own
native beauty.   It is not only cut, carved, honeycombed, perforated, screened, twisted and tortured,
but it is painted, inlaid, gilded and bedizened like
the women, who put huge rings in their nostrils,
metal ornaments through their lips, bracelets on
their arms, anklets on their legs and rings on their
toes.

A school of Art contains a number of boys learning to draw, and to work on metal. It has some fine
specimens of handicraft.

The hotels here and thus far all through India
exhibit a delicious confidence in the honesty of
mankind. The few fastenings which one finds
hardly deserve the name, and a Cooley can rush in
upon you ad libitum. I pleaded last night for a key.
It was promised but came not. Even the latch
would not catch upon the opposite iron and the wind
blew open the door. Nothing remained but to prop

AGRA—THE TAJ-MAHAL.

a chair against it, and trust to Providence. Not to speak of men, the danger from dogs or other animals, is disturbing. Hogs and jackals circulate at liberty.

Permits are required here for visits to the palaces, gardens, etc., but they are freely granted. At the hotel there are printed blanks which require simply your name, date, etc. The Cooley bears the paper to the proper person and brings the permit.

The present Maharajah is a wise and liberal Prince: he has founded schools, a hospital, etc. The streets are lighted with gas. His stables contain 300 horses. We saw no superior animals, nor anything worthy of a visit, although a Gusher had spoken highly of the place. The four ankles of the animals are separately tied, allowing but a few feet of liberty.

AMBER (OR AMBAR) is a suburb of Jeypore. A ride of an hour takes you through several miles of cacti to the foot of a hill. There you mount an elephant and he climbs up and paces down grade for forty minutes more. You go through old gateways, past walls which zig-zag the mountain for miles, through a village which was centuries ago a town enter the stony remnants of old fortifications and at last reach a deserted palace. There is a fine garden. We noticed some pomegranates encased in earthen jars exactly like those our children use for penny, deposit banks. These jars, however, are so divided

that they can be opened and again tied together.
The object is to protect the ripening fruit from the
birds.

There are the usual halls of audience. One of those
at Amber has a more beautiful ceiling than its
counterparts at Delhi or Agra. The Maharajah's
sanctum is lined with little mirrors, reflecting a hundred heads and hands for each reality. Last of all, sad-
dest of all, there was the room of sacrifice to Kale, the
Goddess of Destruction. It is a marble chamber
about twenty feet deep, and forty feet wide. There
are two small pictures of this Destroyer. Three
arches represent places of invocation and a hole
covered with ashes is the spot where for years a
human being was offered every day. When it was
feared that the population could hardly stand this,
a bullock was sacrificed. As these animals became
scarce a goat was substituted. And so it remains.

You meet many peacocks and monkeys enjoying
their wild liberty, and as the night closes 'round
thousands of crows wildly wend their way through
the air seeking shelter in the trees, always preferring
the leafless branches.

Why did the Maharajah in the years gone by for-
sake the beautiful palace we visited and build himself another, almost at the side of the deserted
castle? This was the question we put to the guide.
The answer was suggestive. He said, "simply be-

cause they believe that it is not good luck to live in
the same place more than 500 years."

This ruler we are told has no children. He had
two daughters, but they died.

The weather remains cold (January). Fires in
bed-rooms and overcoat outside save in the glare of
the sun. The thick walls and absence of light give
the chambers the appearance of dungeons. High up,
nine or ten feet above the floor is a sort of transom
sash admitting but a modicum of illumination. Fre-
quently during the day a light is needed to read or
write. Rooms constructed for the fierce heats of summer are rather cheerless when the thermometer is
below 60.

BOMBAY is by rail 699 miles (thirty-three hours)
from Jeypore. The journey requires two nights, with
the usual trouble about refreshments. Hurried
meals and ignorant servants. This trip across India
via Benares, Lucknow, Cawnpore, Agra, Delhi, and
Jeypore is about 1895 miles. The straight line
would be about 1400 miles. Bombay is warm, the
latitude being eighteen degrees north. Philadelphia
time, twelve o'clock noon — here, ten P. M. The
city is located on the sea. In the harbor are many
vessels, some of them ships of war. The islands
make a handsome picture.

The Island of Bombay was given to the English

crown in 1661 by Portugal as part of the dowry of
Catharine of Braganza, but it was not delivered by
the Portuguese until 1665.

In 1668 Charles II sold all his rights in Bombay
to the East India Company for the magnificent sum
of £10 per annum!

The present city was then only an unhealthy
fishing village, but being on an island it was safe
from the cavalry of Mahratta. As Surat had been
raided a few years before, the Western Presidency
was withdrawn from Surat and located at Bombay
in 1687. The population was then about 10,000.
It is now above 800,000; over one-half are Hindoos:
the Mohammedans number 200,000, the Parsees
50,000, the Europeans only about 12,000.

There is a large commingling of many races.
The trade has swollen to 160,000,000 sterling an-
nually. Over one-half of this passes through the
Suez Canal.

The city boasts of many superb buildings. The
Victoria Terminus is one of the finest in the world.
It is of the Italian Gothic style with a front of over
1500 feet. The walls and roof of the interior are
decorated with blue and gold. The Administrative
office building occupies three sides of a square with
a fine garden. A high tower rises over the centre
surmounted by a figure representing Progress. A
statue of the Empress-Queen is in front of the
building.

BLUNDI BAZAAR, BOMBAY.

THE ROYAL ALFRED SAILORS' HOME is well worthy of notice. I have not the means of comparing it with the Home at Liverpool, but both are splendid institutions. The Bombay building seems to be the larger of the two. It is a beautiful structure and was completed in 1876. Its object is to secure a shelter for sailors. Here they are safe from the boarding house plunderers. The cost to each sailor is only one rupee (about twenty-five cents) a day. Officers pay thirty-eight cents a day. The lot is about three acres; the building is fire-proof throughout. There is a fine library and reading room. Boards for draughts and chess are supplied. There are dining rooms, bath-rooms and every comfort. The establishment can accommodate five hundred. The ship-wrecked and distressed are entertained free of charge.

THE CAVES OF ELEPHANTA are lauded by travellers as objects of special attraction. They are not worth the trouble and expense of a visit. They are on an island sometimes called Gharapuri (the hill of Purification) and again Garrapuri (the city of Excavations). Years ago a stone elephant stood on a hill near by, and the Portuguese called the island Elaphanta. The statue has long since been removed and is now in the Victoria Gardens. The island is about seven miles from Bombay. A little steamer

carries you there in
about an hour. You
must, however, get into
a small boat and be
rocked and wet and
rowed some five min-
utes to a curious land-
ing, composed of con-
crete blocks extending
far out into the bay.
Mounting on these a
walk of five minutes
takes you to a fearful
succession of stone steps
l e a d i n g considerably
over a quarter of a mile
up an ascent of over one
hundred and fifty feet.

Here you must pay
another fee to enter the
sacred ground. A few
feet bring you to a hall
cut out of the black
rock, some say 133 feet
by 130 feet. Others say
ninety feet square. It
rests on pillars from
fifteen to seventeen feet
in height. Instead of

A HINDOO BRAHMIN GIRL.

being of considerable elegance, they are without a
particle of attraction. There is a three-headed
figure on the wall, said to represent Shiv in the
character of Brahma—Shiv as Rudra the destroyer.
This is embellished with a swelling above the nose,
said to represent a third eye. And the third face is
called Shiv in the character of Vishnu, the pre-
server. Cobras and a human skull are cut. It is
stated that "the royal tiara is most beautifully
carved," and that the "face has a stern, commanding Roman expression." But this is all imagination. There is nothing beautiful or commanding
about any of the figures. An apartment to the left
and a chamber on the other side contain equally
hideous carvings, all without a particle of symmetry
or attraction. It is said that these were cut 1200
years ago. This is probably the only truth stated
by guide books and frothy writers.

The view of the city and the bay was the only
return for an afternoon lost and five rupees spent.

THE TOWERS OF SILENCE are also represented as
an attraction. The drive occupies an hour. On
Malabar Hill you have a splendid view of Bombay
and the sea. This is all of your return. You enter
gates, climb a hill and are received by a Parsee into
a large area, said to be of 75,000 square yards.
There is nothing wonderful here. A small stone

building is used for prayer and service over the
dead; it can not be called a burial service. Then
there are five structures called towers but they are
not towers in any proper sense of the word. They
are square, ugly-looking affairs about twenty-five
feet in height, with an entrance at the end of an

LUCKNOW—THE MARTINIÉRE.

elevated road, about half way to the top. It is said
that the dead are carried inside and placed in rows.
In every building there are 216 ledges in three
circles of seventy-two each, all side by side, not one
above the other. Seventy-two are for male adults,
these are in the circle next to the walls, seventy-two

for female adults in the second circle, and seventy-
two for children in the centre circle. The five
towers can therefore accommodate 1080 bodies. In
the centre of each is a well. The bodies are left
exposed: the vultures strip them of their flesh
and then the bones are thrown into the well. One
is shown a wooden model of a single building and
then he goes away slightly nauseated. We were
told that two bodies had been carried into the
building pointed out to us a few hours before. On
the top were half a dozen vultures. Imagination
supplied the horrid, disgusting, cruel blank.

The public buildings speak well for English taste
and enterprise. The University Hall, the Yacht
Club, the Schools, Police Courts, Post Office and the
Secretariat are all structures of which any city
might be proud.

PINJRAROOT is the name of a new market in which
are hospital enclosures for lame and sick animals,
who are fed and tenderly cared for. The Hindoo
deserves all praise for his mercy to beasts. Lame
bullocks, wounded cows, homeless dogs, and even
sick pigeons, find a refuge here.

A large proportion of the colored population in
Bombay are Parsees. They seem to be wealthy,
enterprising and benevolent citizens. Their schools

merit high commendation. Their dress is European
with the exception of the Persian hat.

The poverty of the lower classes, and the climate,

A PARSEE PRIEST.

account for the number of bare feet and bare legs
seen amongst the Hindoos. Of the men, it seemed
to me, 90 per cent. were more or less naked from
the hips down. One third of these denuded males

wear nothing below the thighs. Some of them
have only a girdle. A large number however wear
a sort of a petticoat or apron which comes below the

A PARSEE LADY.

knee, but is then turned backwards to the waist behind. This arrangement covers the greater part of
the limbs in front, but leaves the rear of the legs

almost entirely nude. The women are, as a general
thing, all covered, a large percentage however have

A BRAHMIN WOMAN.

bare feet and many of them sport rings on their toes.
Some of the sex are more exposed. When one is
12

walking through a narrow and crowded thoroughfare swarming with these brown skins, some in
part unclothed, others shining in brilliant colors,
it is a picture which pen can hardly paint and
which reminds you of a kaleidoscope.

The weather here in January is delightful. Open
doors and windows, with fine sea breezes. It seems
a happy escape from the fierce storms and biting
cold, the sneezing, wheezing, and coughing of
Philadelphia.

The curious names seen on signs, and on the
street corners, are illustrated by a few specimens:

Sabapathy Moodeliar & Co., Bank St.

Shagwan Dass Hurjeevan & Co., Custom House
Road.

B. W. Pathuck, Tamarind Lane.

Cowasjee Brother, Cowasjee Patel St.

Cursetjee Muncherjee Bhesenia & Co., Hornby Rd.

Currimbhoy Ebrahim & Co., Khoja Mohulla.

Dinthaw D. Currance & Co., Cowesjee Patel St.

Dorabjee Shapoorjee & Co., Elphintstone Circle.

Hamshedjee Nusserwanjee Tata, Paree Mazaar St.

Merwanjee Nusserwanjee Sons & Co., Medows St.

Mooljee Jaitha & Co., Tamarind Lane.

Muncherjee Nowrojee Banajee & Co., Hornby Rd.

Mansukhlall, Demodar & Jumsetjee, Medows St.

Nusserwanjee Bomanjee Mody & Co., Hornby Rd.

Nanabhoy B. Jajeebhoy & Co., Hornby Rd.

N. S. Pochajee & Co., Custom House Rd.
N. V. Currance & Co., Custom House Rd.
Pestanjee, Rustim & Kola, Medows St.
Purshotam Bandoojee & Co., Medows St.
R. Ranchandra & Co., Forbes St.
Ruttonsey, Denso & Co., Elphinstone Circle.
Sorabjee Shapoorjee & Co., Medows St.
Sorabshah & Co., Medows St.
Tata & Sons, Parsee Bazaar St.
Tanidass Vurjdass & Co., Dalal St.
Thakurdaas Dharamsi & Co., Esplanade Rd.
Tharic Topun, Samuel St.
Tyabjee & Co., Humnum St.
Visram Ebrahim & Co., Samuel St.

THE CYCLONES.—In the Autumn terrible storms
have been known to inflict fearful disasters. All the
Eastern shore of India is exposed to these visitations. A history of them has been given by Mr.
Lanier in his excellent work, "Asia." He describes
the storm of October 31, 1876, as destroying in one
hour and without warning, 215,000 lives, each city
losing 70 per cent. of its population. This was followed by the cholera.

HOMEWARD BOUND.

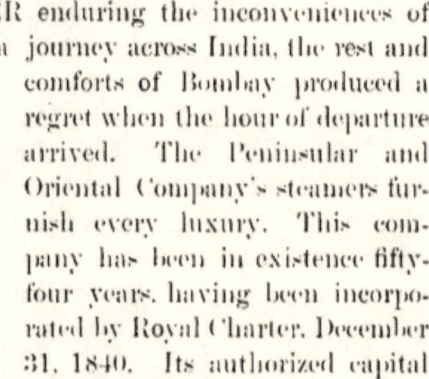

AFTER enduring the inconveniences of a journey across India, the rest and comforts of Bombay produced a regret when the hour of departure arrived. The Peninsular and Oriental Company's steamers furnish every luxury. This company has been in existence fifty-four years, having been incorporated by Royal Charter, December 31, 1840. Its authorized capital is £3,500,000, of which there has been issued and paid up, £2,320,000. It owns a fleet of fifty-one ships, and has now in course of construction seven more vessels. Besides these there are twenty-three tugs and launches, making a total tonnage of 259,593 tons, with 243,545 effective horse power. Its management is composed of the best men, and the results are most gratifying. The receipts for 1894 were over £2,300,000, on which dividends equal to 5 per cent. on the preferred, and 10 per cent. on the deferred stock were distributed. The coal preferred is the Welsh. Its average cost, the year round, counting freight, etc., is from twenty to twenty-five shilling a ton. The Peninsular burns about sixty-five tons a day. The largest boat, "The Caledonian," consumes eighty tons a day. These boats pay tolls on the Suez canal, at the rate of eight francs a ton, and twenty-five francs a head. This company paid to the Suez Company in 1894, over a million of dollars. From Bombay to Aden is 1660 miles. The voyage took four days and thirteen hours. Aden is a coaling port at the southwest corner of Arabia. The mountains rise all round it very abruptly and the summits are bare and rugged. It is said that the rain only falls once in three years. Here the old Romans had a settlement and traces of their civilization still exist. The Gulf of Aden leads to the straits of Babel-mendeb. This is Arabic, it seems, for the "Gate of Weeping." It is the entrance to the Red Sea, abounding in shoals. The navigation was so disastrous that the ancients gave to the entrance this poetical name. The Strait is only about one mile in width. To the left on an eminence stands Perim, also controlled by the British. Marvelous and far-reaching power! Away from the breezes, the air is very hot. Awnings on deck and punkas in the cabin keep one happy. The Lascars compose the working crews of these vessels. They are inhabitants of India, to the south of Bombay, are very

dark, generally wear beards, always have red tur-
bans and look very savage. They are described as
teachable, but the slowness with which they got a
boat uncovered and swung it to the side, seemed
almost comical. Instead of compelling them to
learn English, the poor officers are forced to learn
the dialect of their seamen. When I asked why
ordinary Hindoos were not hired, the captain told
me they would lose caste if they came to sea. The
first-class fare from Bombay to Brindisi is $175.
From Brindisi to London, including sleeping car, is
$74. As this latter takes only two days, it seems to
be the highest rate known.

The distances are:

Bombay to Aden	1660 Miles.
Aden to Ismailia .	1356 "
Ismalia to Port Said .	43 "
Port Said to Brindisi	930 "
	—— "
	3989 "
Brindisi to London (by rail and	
channel boat) . . .	1450
	——
	5439

SUEZ.—On the fourth day you reach Suez, 1309
miles from Aden. In the Bay you pass Sinai, and
further on, one of the places assigned by tradition as
the crossing of the Israelites. Still another spot is
fixed for this great miracle up near Bitter Lake, in-

side of the canal. Suez, once a great place for trade,
has of course lost its importance since the construction of the canal. Great credit is due to de Lesseps
and his associates for their courage and perseverance
in this behalf. But the truth is, that a canal ex-
isted as far back as the reign of Pharaoh Necho,
and the five lakes which form part of the passage
reduced the prestige of a work at most but ninety-
eight miles in extent. Lord Palmerston was at heart
against the enterprise; he wisely feared political com-
plications. But though liberal in profession he was
ever asking, what is the use? and how can this be
avoided? In this spirit he commissioned two eminent
engineers to examine the whole scheme. They em-
balmed themselves in history by a report that the
canal was impracticable and that the Mediterranean
was two feet and some inches above the Red Sea, a de-
duction absolutely negatived by the fact. The canal
was finished in 1868 despite these prophecies. Years
afterwards D'Israeli, acting under the interested but
able advice of Rothschild secured a grand result for
Great Britain by purchasing the stock at 80. These
and many other interesting items were given to me
by Captain Briscoe, of "The Peninsular," who many
years ago showed his faith in the enterprise by in-
vesting his savings in the stock when low down at
20. The result has proved his sagacity to be superior
to English statesmen and engineers, for the shares

now command, he says, 120. The entrance of the
canal, called Port Tewfik, two and a half miles
from Suez, is marked by two buoys and the whole
channel is staked. At night it is all lighted. The
only place of interest in the neighborhood is in Asia,
about two miles from Suez. It is called "The Wells
of Moses," and is reached by crossing the canal and
by a ride on a donkey. On either side Arabia and
Egypt vie in their display of long, low stretches of
desert. Here and there is a village, or a camp of
Arabs and camels. Occasionally there is a pretty
station with a palm tree, the rest is a desolation,
marked only by buoys, little gas tanks to illuminate
the channel; men and camels engaged in cutting off
corners and small posts marking the miles and tenths
of miles. Vessels may follow; two are astern as I
write, but passing abreast, both in motion is not allowed. One ship must tie up. The channel is very
narrow, in places not over 150 feet in width and is
shallow. At the sides of the passage a few feet of
water cover shoals visible to the eye and the banks
are lined with stone walls and little palisades to protect from the wash. Dredgers are also employed.
The time usually consumed in passing from Suez to
Port Said is fifteen hours. Of course an accident
may obstruct commerce for some time. A passenger
told me that he had been delayed here four days.

ISMAILIA is on Lake Timsah half way between Suez and Port Said. Travellers can land at Suez, and take the rail to Ismailia (three hours) and thence to Cairo about four hours. Or as the time table may require, they can leave the boat at Ismailia. The majority prefer this plan. The rail also runs to Alexandria, three hours to Cairo by the fast line.

PORT SAID is about seven hours by boat from Ismailia. It is the northern terminus of the canal and its little area is owned in strips by several sovereignties. It is remarkable only for its splendid breakwaters and its vices.

CANDIA.—On the second day from Port Said we passed a little to the south of Candia (Crete). This beautiful island is 160 miles long and for several hours we looked with admiration on its high mountains covered with snow. The light of the setting sun made them the handsomest object seen in a very long voyage. Here Paul sailed and crossed to the little Island of Claudia.

ZANTE.—Remarkable for currants and earthquakes. Cephalonia and other islands were passed on the third day from Port Said. We are due this midnight at Brindisi, nearly thirteen days from Bombay. All over these routes the stoppages seem timed for unwelcome hours. Those who land and

those who remain are alike tortured by these untimely arrivals.

From Brindisi to London the overland mail takes
about fifty hours.

HISTORIC SKETCH OF THE ANGLO-INDIAN
EMPIRE.

The effective control of a domain of vast territorial extent, containing a population of over 200
millions, perhaps a full sixth of that of the entire
globe, by a people utterly inferior in point of numbers, and whose seat is at the remote Antipodes, is a
phenomenon which, both in its historic and sociologi-
cal aspects, is singular and striking. Apart from its
political significance, the growing importance of
British India as a factor in the world's affairs and
its increasing influence on economic conditions in
this country, will make a brief review of the development of British rule in India of interest to
every American reader. The following historic
sketch has accordingly been condensed for these
pages from the lucid recital, by W. W. Hunter, in
his "Brief History of the Indian People."

The first territorial possession of the English on
the mainland of the Indian peninsula was Fort St.

George, now Madras, founded by Francis Day in
1639. The French settlement of Pondicherri, about
one hundred miles farther down the east or Coro-
mandel coast, was established in 1674, and for about
seventy years the two races lived and traded peaceably together. The war between England and
France in 1744 broke this long peace. Dupleix,
one of the ablest Frenchmen of his time was
Governor of Pondicherri. The other great actor in
Indian history, Clive, the Englishman, was then in
a business office, at Madras. An English fleet first
put in an appearance, but Dupleix by skillful
diplomacy induced the native prince, the Nawab of
Arcot, to prevent hostilities. In 1746 a French
fleet appeared and Madras surrendered almost without a blow, leaving Fort St. David, some miles
south of Pondicherri, the only fort held by the
English race in India. Here Clive and a few other
fugitives sought shelter. The Nawab, endeavoring
to be entirely impartial sought to drive out the
French but was defeated. In 1768 an English fleet
under Boscawen laid siege to Pondicherri aided by
an army under Lawrence, but unsuccessfully. The
treaty of Aix-la-Chappelle, however, restored
Madras to the English.

The second war between the French and English
in India had no reference to European complica-
tions. Disputed successions among the native

princes gave Dupleix the chance of becoming
arbiter, who by this means hoped to erect a great
French empire in India. Had Dupleix been as
great in the field as he was able and bold in
diplomacy history for the 200,000,000 of India
would have been different. It was, however, the
good fortune of the English to have a series of able
soldiers, the chief of whom was Lord Clive. The
capture and defence of Arcot by Clive in 1751, the
battle of Wandewash, won by Sir Eyre Coote in
1760 and the capture of Pondicherri by the same
soldier in 1761 ended forever the dream of Dupleix
of founding an empire in India. This was the close
of the war between the English and French in India,
brought about by their support of rival candidates
for the throne of Arcot. The next steps for the
foundation of English supremacy were taken against
the native princes, the scene shifting with Clive to
Bengal, the northern part of India.

The war in Bengal, of which the famous battle of
Plassey (1757) was the turning point, began like
the war of 1746, in the fact of the French and English
being at war with each other in Europe. Clive
captured the French settlement of Chandarnagar on
the Hoogli River, near Calcutta. This was within
the domains of the Nawab of Bengal, Surajah Daw-
lah, the man responsible for the "Black Hole" epi-
sode of Calcutta, in 1756. Outraged at this violation

of neutrality the Nawab sided with the French. Clive marched to the grove of Plassey, seventy miles from Calcutta, with a force of 1000 Europeans, 2000 Sepoys and eight pieces of artillery. The Nawab is said to have had 35,000 foot, 15,000 cavalry and fifty guns. He attacked with his whole artillery at six in the morning. Clive, knowing his inferiority in this respect kept his men well sheltered "in a grove, surrounded with good mud banks." At noon, the Nawab's men drew off for dinner, feeling, no doubt, perfectly safe in their vast superiority of numbers and equipment. Whilst at dinner, Clive attacked one of their outposts, and stormed "an angle of the camp." Several leading officers of the Nawab fell and the latter, surprised at the confusion, fled, his troops flying in panic. Clive, no doubt, as much surprised as any, found himself winner of a great victory, and the British Empire in India was born. This day was June 23, 1757, an anniversary celebrated 100 years later by the blood and terror of the revolt of the Sepoys in 1857.

In 1758, Clive was appointed by the East India Company the first governor of all its settlements in Bengal. Though Plassey is generally deemed to have given birth to the Indian Empire, yet years of toil and bloodshed were yet to come before it should be firmly founded. Indeed, it may be said, not to have been absolutely entrenched until after the Se-

poy mutiny of 1857. Clive found two wars threatened immediatly upon his accession to the governor-
ship, one by the Shahzada, or, as he was called afterwards, the Emperor Shah Alam, the other by the
French at Madras. The former leading an army of
Afghans and Mahrattas, and supported by the
Nawab of Oudh, asserted his claim, as Emperor, to
the province of Bengal and laid siege to Patna, an
important post about 600 miles northwest of Calcutta. Clive marched in person to the rescue, with
the ridiculously small force of 450 Europeans and
2500 Sepoys; yet so great was the terror of his very
name that the Mogul army dispersed without waiting
to be attacked. In the south, Colonel Forde recaptured
Masilupatam from the French, and permantly established English authority at Hyderabad and through
the northern Circars. Clive in person attacked the
Dutch and defeated them, both on land and sea, and
rendered them utterly unable to rival the English,
to aid the French, or even hold their own settlements, or anything else than the sufferance of the
victors.

From 1760 to 1765 Clive was in England and a
war sprung up in his absence. Mir Jafar, whom
the English had just put as their puppet upon the
viceregal throne of Murshidabad to succeed the
Siraj-ud-Daula (or Surajah Dowlah), after the
defeat of the latter at Plassey, as already described,

was displaced and Mir Kasim, his son-in-law, was
seated in his throne. The latter proceeded to in-
trigue with the Nawab of Oudh, already mentioned,
and to organize a force on the English model, with
the hope of trying conclusions with the latter. A
quarrel over the inland duties in Bengal afforded
the excuse, the natives refusing to pay to the Nawab's officers on the ground that they (the natives)
were acting for the English company. The Nawab's men massacred 2000 Sepoys at Patna and
some hundreds of Europeans who fell into their
hands there and in other parts of the province. In
pitched battles, however, Mir Kasim's trained regiments were utterly defeated by Major Adams at
Gheriah and Udha-nala and the leader took refuge
with the Nawab of Oudh. To add to the difficulties
of the English, the first Sepoy mutiny broke out in
their camp. It was quelled by Sir Hector Munro
and twenty-four ringleaders were blown from the
mouths of cannon, this being an old Mogul form of
punishment. The war ended by Sir Hector's decis-
ive victory at Baxar in 1764, which laid Oudh at
the feet of the English and brought the Mogul Emperor, himself, Shah Alam (already mentioned as
the prince Shahzada) a suppliant to the camp of the
conquerors.

In 1765 Clive returned to India as Governor of
Bengal. He restored Oudh to the Nawab for half

a million sterling, toward war expenses. A puppet
was maintained at Murshidabad and the fiscal administration only of Bengal, Behar and Orissa, as
well as the territorial jurisdiction of the Northern
Circars was given to the East Indian Company. A
task much greater for Clive, however, was the re-or-
ganization of the Civil Service of the company.
This was brought about by an increase in salaries
and a prohibition to all officers from engaging in
private trade and from receiving presents (that is,
bids) from the native powers. Clive returned to
England finally in 1767.

The great famine of 1770, in which it is said that
one third of the people of India perished, was the
only great event between this date and the governor-
ship of the famous Warren Hastings, beginning in
1772. Clive's double system of control already
adverted to was shown to be a failure. The puppet
Nawab of Murshidabad had received an allowance
from the English of 600,000 pounds sterling, when
first appointed by Clive. The latter before leaving
India had himself cut this enormous sum down to
450,000 pounds, in 1766, on the accession of a new
Nawab, and to 350,000 pounds on a fresh succession
in 1769. Six months before Clive became governor,
the Court of Directors of the East India Company
had ordered the sum cut down about one-half, or to
about 160,000 pounds. Hastings carried this order

out, though in his famous trial before the English Parliament, this was charged against him, as an act of oppression and of treaty breaking as to the Nawab. Another act of Hastings was the sale of Allahabad and Kora to the Wazir of Oudh.

The provinces had been assigned to the Emperor Shah Alam, already mentioned together with a tribute of 300,000 pounds sterling in return for the grant of Bengal to the English. Shortly after this grant the Marhattas, a warlike northern race, had attacked the Emperor and seized his person. Hastings held that this destroyed the Emperor's independence and that it would be folly to continue paying tribute to have it fall into the hands of the Marhattas, thus strengthening their hands against the time when the English should have to fight them. He therefore withheld the tribute. He also resold Allahabad and Kora to the Wazir of Oudh for half a million sterling and at the same time freed the company of a military burden of nearly as much more, making a saving in Indian finances of nearly five million dollars per annum. Chait Sinh, the Rajah of Benares, revolted, and his estates were forfeited; the Begum, or Queen Mother of Oudh, on a charge of abetting him was also fined to the extent of one million sterling. Hastings' trial before the Lords for these and other acts of oppression lasting

13

from 1788 to 1795, was one of the greatest state
trials of history.

It resulted in his acquittal but left him ruined.
The excuse offered for Warren Hastings' course was
that he had to fight for life against princes who broke
faith with him and that he used his power more
mercifully than any Mogul Viceroy would have
done. That he was the greatest man that ever ruled
India is now universally admitted.

The Marhatta war of 1778–1781 was signalized
by brave acts, but beyond this seems to have been
entirely fruitless. The war with Hyder Ali, of
Mysore and the Nizam of the Deccan, the two
strongest Mohammedan powers in India, was almost
disastrous to the English. Hyder cut several English
forces to pieces and ravaged the Karnatic, an English
province, so that it was said not a living thing remained in it. Hyder was an able soldier and,
when he died in 1782, peace was concluded with
his son by mutual restitution of all conquests.

Lord Cornwallis was twice governor general, first
from 1786 to 1793 and again in 1805. He improved and built upon the foundations of civil
administration laid by Hastings, first gave criminal
jurisdiction to Europeans and carried into execution
the permanent settlement of the land tax for Bengal. In the second Mysore war with Tipu Sultan,
son of Hyder Ali (1790-1792), Lord Cornwallis led

in person, conquering from the enemy one-half of his possessions and exacting tribute of three millions sterling.

Sir John Shore (afterward Lord Teignmouth) was governor-general from 1793 to 1798, and was succeeded by Lord Mornington, better known as the Marquis of Wellesley. He is credited with laying down the Imperial policy of India, viz: that England should be the one paramount power and that native princes should only be permitted to reign by surrendering their political independence. The logical and final result of this was the proclamation of Victoria as Empress of India, on January 1, 1877. Wellesly bought the Doab, a fertile province, from the Nawab Wazir of Oudh in consideration of the unpaid balance of subsidies owed by the latter to the English. He entered into treaty with the Nizam of Hyderabad and without bloodshed turned him into an ally. He also made him promise to employ no Europeans without English consent, a provision aimed to destroy the French influence at the Nizam's Court. Tippoo, the Sultan of Mysore, had intrigued with the French and war was declared against him. As became a soldier and a king he died in the trench at the storming of Seringapatam, 1799. His estates were divided between the English, their native allies and an infant Hindu prince whose ancestors had been robbed by Tippoo's father,

the Great Hyder Ali. Tippoo's sons were treated
with the greatest kindness, and the last of his
descendants died, a magistrate at Calcutta, in 1877.
After this the English devoted their attention to the
loose Marhatta Confederacy, the third power of
Southern India. The second Marhatta War (1802–
1803) followed, said to be the most glorious chapter
in the English Wars in India, though there were
some disasters, as in the first war with Hyder Ali in
Mysore. In Northwestern India, Lord Lake's cam-
paigns brought the northwest provinces under
English rule together with the old Emperor, the
puppet successor of the Great Mogul. This office of
Emperor actually maintained a shadowy existence
at Delhi till 1857, the Sepoy revolt.

In 1805 Lord Cornwallis was again sent to India,
but died at Ghazipur before having been ten weeks
in the country. Sir George Barlow succeeded during a few months. During his term another mutiny
of Sepoys occurred at Vellore (1806). It was brief
and promptly suppressed but sent a feeling of
insecurity through the empire. Lord Minto,
governor-general from 1807 to 1813, was distinguished by few military operations, though the
governor managed to consolidate Wellesley's conquests and keep the peace without sacrificing
English prestige.

The successor of Lord Minto was the Earl of

Moira, better known as Marquis of Hastings (1814-1823). Two wars of the first magnitude and the suppression of the free-booting Pindaris, in Central India, characterize this period. The first war was with the hardy little Goorkhas, in Nepaul, in 1814-15, in which the English, at first fairly beaten, finally succeeded in obtaining their own terms. The other was with the Marhattas and resulted in the final subjection of these war-like people, and the giving of orderly and good government to their wretched retainers. The war against the Pindaris was of an altogether different character. These people were not a race like the Marhattas nor were they bound together by purely religious ties, as the Sikhs. They were merely plundering bands, like the free companies of mediaeval Europe, with no community of race or religious sentiment. They preyed over much of Central India from Madras to Bombay and one of their chiefs had an organized army of many regiments and considerable artillery. Lord Hastings collected 120,000 men to operate against them and they were finally completely overcome.

Lord Amherst ruled from 1823 to 1828 and had two wars to carry on, the first Burmese campaign and the capture of Bhurtpoor. The Burmese War (1824–26) was forced on the English by Burmese raids and the refusal of the raiders to con-

sider any peaceful proposals. It cost the English
the lives of 20,000 men and $70,000,000 and
resulted in the cession of two provinces. Bhurtpoor
was taken by Lord Combermere in 1827 by storm,
though a similar attempt in 1805 had resulted
disastrously to the English.

Lord William Bentinck, a descendant of the famous Bentinck, Duke of Portland, the friend and
counsellor of William of Orange, was governor from
1828 to 1835. But little war characterized his administration; but it is to his imperishable glory
that during his rule Lord Bentinck began the course
of administrative and other reform which have
made modern India and its millions happier and
better than ever in their history. He equalized
taxes, encouraged educated natives to enter the service of the English, and abolished the burning of
widows and the murders of the thugs. The burning of widows, it was claimed, was in obedience to a
text in the Vedic hymns, written in the tongue
which is the common parent of Hindostanee, Greek,
Latin, Lithuanian and English. But modern schol-
arship had clearly shown that this use of the text
was the result of a mistranslation. The result of
this move on the part of the governor general has
shed most distinguished honor on the English
name. In 1834, the misrule of the Raja of Coorg
brought on a short, sharp war, the natives wishing to

be taken under English protection. This was done and the Rajah retired to Benares. This was the only annexation during Lord Bentinck's administration, and it was done "in consideration of the unanimous wish of the people."

Sir Charles (afterward Lord) Metcalfe was governor general in 1835–36. His administration was memorable for the bestowal of full liberty to the native press, a measure initiated by his predecessor.

With Lord Metcalfe's successor, Lord Auckland (1836–42) begins another chapter of war, not always honorable or creditable to England. The active interference in Afghan politics dates from Lord Auckland's sending an army to Kabul, the Afghan capital, to put Shah Shuja on the throne (1839). The English army remained for two years; but in November, 1841, the English political agent, Sir Alexander Burnes, was assassinated, as was also Sir William Menaghten. After a delay of two months the British Army set out in midwinter to return to India. Of the 4000 fighting men and 12,000 camp followers, just one man, Dr. Brydon, reached Jalalabad. A few prisoners were taken and well treated by orders of Akbar Khan, eldest son of Dost Mohammed, whom the English had dethroned to put up Shah Shuja.

The garrison of Kandahar, the old capital of Afghanistan, abandoned that city and coming home

by way of Kabul, met there the army which had
been sent to relieve Jalalabad but had gone as far as
Kabul. The English contented themselves with
blowing up the bazaar at Kabul and recovering the
English prisoners and then returned to India, leaving Dost Mohammed on the throne where he was
before their intervention. The withdrawal of the
garrisons was the work of Lord Ellenborough, who
succeeded Lord Auckland about a month after the
news of the annihilation of the army retreating
from Kabul reached Calcutta (1842). The conquest
of the Ameers of Sindh, a most unjust war, and the
war against Gwalior were the two other wars of Lord
Ellenborough's career.

Sir Henry Hardinge, a veteran of Napoleon's wars,
who had lost a hand at Ligny just before Waterloo,
succeeded Elenborough, governing from 1844 to
1848. His administration was characterized by the
conquest of the great Sikh nation, who, as already said,
were a great religious sect, whose history, teachings,
and unflinching courage were alike remarkable. The
great Ranjit Sinh, founder of the political power of the
Sikhs, had organized his fellows into regiments upon
a religious basis, similar to that of Gustavus Adol-
phus and Cromwell, and had extended his conquests
far and wide over the extreme north of India. He was
also strictly faithful to his word as given to the
English. After Ranjit's death, however, a different

state of things arose. In 1845 a Sikh army of
60,000 men with 150 guns crossed the then bound-
ary, the Sutlej river, and invaded India. Sir Hugh
Gough, English commander, fought four desperate
battles with them, with heavy loss. In the end,
however, Lahore, the Sikh capital, was taken. Sir
Henry Lawrence was sent there as resident, a portion of their territory annexed and a British garrison
occupied the Punjab for eight years.

The Earl of Dalhousie (1848–1856) is said to have
left a greater impression upon India than any man
since the days of Clive. Whilst it is true that he
was compelled to fight with the Sikhs and Burmah
and to annex large territories, his deepest concerns
were for the material and moral welfare of the people. He it was who gave the first impetus to the
network of railroads and canals which, by making
communication easy, has rendered famines almost
impossible; he it was who encouraged telegraphs
and steamship lines and means of improvement.
He had not been six months in India before the
second Sikh war (1848–49) broke out. The English
lost at the battle of Chilianwala 2400 men, four
guns and three regimental colors, January 13,
1849. Lord Gough, however, redeemed himself at
Gujrat, where he entirely destroyed the Sikh force.
The Punjab was annexed by proclamation of 29th
of March, 1849. The Rajah, Dhulip Sinh, was

given a pension of £58,000 and lived comfortably in England.

The means taken to pacificate the country were so effective that the Sikhs were absolutely faithful to the English when half India was ablaze during the terrible mutiny soon to come. Taxes were reduced, equitable laws introduced and enforced, evenhanded justice meted out to the people and peace and prosperity followed. The second Burmese war, following the ill-treatment of some English merchants at Rangoon, resulted (1852) in the annexation of a large part of the valley of the Irawadi. Here, too, the effect of orderly government was soon seen. The trade of Rangoon increased four-fold in twenty-five years and its population has been multiplied by ten since annexation. Lord Dalhousie acted throughout on the theory that the good of the governed was the purpose of government; and in pursuance of this idea, whilst rigorously respecting the rights of reigning princes, invariably annexed possessions in which the incumbent had died leaving no natural heir. This was done, too, even in the cases in which the princes sought to over-reach the English by adopting heirs to the inheritances. Oudh was also annexed in 1856, and the king was given an annual pension of $600,000. The orders to Sir James Outram, the resident, were to assume the administration, on the ground that "the British Government would be guilty in the sight of God and man if it were any longer to aid in sustaining by its countenance an administration fraught with suffering to millions;" this was in reference to the rule of the native prince whom the English thus finally displaced. The annexation was only decided upon after repeated warnings to the Nawabs, extending over a long series of years, that they must govern justly and humanely or suffer the consequences. The irony of fate was such, however, that these very acts of humanity and amelioration were probably leading causes in the great revolt of the following year.

The appointment of Earl Canning (1856-62) was soon followed by the terrible mutiny of 1857, the last great tragedy in the long, checkered, but in the main, highly honorable career of England in India. It seems singular, that even to this day, the exact cause of this great tragedy is not known. It is probable, as already remarked, that the spread of civilization and of Western reforms had the effect of alarming Hindoo public opinion and of conveying the impression that their nationalities and religions were in danger. The introduction of rifles into the army required the use of lubricated paper envelope cartridges, which, before being loaded, had to be bitten off on the end. The report that the lubricating

material was hog's lard, was the match that set fire
to the magazine. On Sunday, May 10, 1857, the
storm broke at Meerut, where the native troops cut
down the English officers and all the Europeans
they could find, and rushed off to the nearby town
of Delhi, to put themselves under the authority of
the old man who still claimed the shadowy title of
Emperor of the Mogul Empire of India. The same
terrible scenes, including also, in many cases, mas-
sacres of English women and children, were enacted
in many other places. The native armies of Madras
and Bombay remained true to the English, and the
Sikh population of the Punjab, recently conquered,
poured out *en masse* to aid the English.

Cawnpore, Lucknow and Delhi were the chief
centres of interest. At the first named, the English portion of the garrison after a desperate resist-
ance of nineteen days under a tropical June sky,
surrendered and were promised a safe conduct as
far as Allahabad, down the Ganges. They had no
sooner embarked than fire was opened on them and
of 450, only four escaped (June 27, 1857). 125
women and children who were left behind were
massacred a few weeks later (July 15). At Lucknow,
Sir Henry Lawrence had foreseen the storm and
chosen his defences. The garrison held out under
terrible hardships and against heavy odds from July
2d to September 25, when relieved by Havelock

and Outram.   The combined force was besieged till
November 16th, when finally relieved by Sir Colin
Campbell (Lord Clyde).   The garrison then retired
to places where they were more urgently needed.
Delhi was besieged by a force of 8000 Englishmen
against 30,000 Sepoys, beginning on June 8th.   In
August, General Nicholson arrived with reinforce-
ments from the Punjab, and after a desperate assault
of six days, Delhi fell on September 20th.   After
this, the war decreased in interest, though it lasted
in places for nearly two years longer.   The war in
Oudh was carried on by Sir Colin Campbell aided
by Sir Jang Bahadur of Nepal at the head of the
gallant little Gurkhas.   Central India was reduced
by Sir Hugh Rose (afterward Lord Strathnairn) and
here some of the most tragic and romantic scenes
were enacted.

Here it was that the Princess of Jhansi died in
battle at the head of her troops in June, 1858, and
here it was that Sir Hugh put again in practice
the old Mogul punishment of blowing insurgents
from the mouths of cannon.   Much hostile criticism
has been directed against the English for these
things; yet there is little doubt that such determined
acts, such a utilization of native fears and super-
stitions as was contained in these executions, served
to bring the war to a close, to save much bloodshed
and to give England a firmer grasp on her Indian

possessions. That she should ever give them up is
not to be thought of, and that she may never do so
is the devout wish of every one who realizes what
blessings of peace, order and justice have resulted to
those teeming millions from her rule. The end of
the mutiny also marked the end of the East India
Company, all of whose powers were transferred to
the crown in 1858, after an existence of 258 years.

Since the mutiny no internecine troubles of any
consequence have occurred. Reforms have gone
steadily forward and the conquerors have shown
more than once their ability to cope with famine
and to some extent with pestilence. During the
viceroyalty of Lord Northbrook (1872–76) a famine
which threatened Lower Bengal in 1874 was successfully averted. In 1878 the government despite
tremendous efforts was not quite so successful.
A general drought over most of the Empire
caused crop failures, and over five millions perished.
Much of this result is due to the peculiar habits of
the people themselves. A large proportion of them
will not eat flesh food. As they will not even slay
animals, many forms of animal life are so plentiful
that enormous quantities of food fit for human
beings are destroyed in consequence. The natives
are also so intensely conservative that they cannot
be induced to leave over populated districts for
localities where land can be had for the asking.

But with all these drawbacks, the population of India is increasing with strides so enormous that this, in turn, is becoming a great social question.

In 1878 the affairs of Afghanistan forced themselves to the attention of the English government. Shere Ali, the Ameer, was found to be favoring the Russians, whilst declining to receive an English envoy. This lead to war. Three British armies entered the three great Himalayan passes and Shere Ali fled. His son, Yakub Khan, made a treaty, advancing the British boundaries and admitting an English envoy. Within a few months, this officer, Major Louis Cavagnari, was murdered and a second war promptly followed. Kabul and Kandahar were occupied and Yakub Khan was deported to India. A force sent into Afghanistan by Ayoub Khan was also brilliantly repulsed by Sir Frederick Roberts, September 1, 1880. Abdurrahman Khan was subsequently recognized as Ameer and is now on the throne. The British forces retired in March, 1881.

The main features of the present condition of British India are its industrial and economic elements. The constant friction between the Hindoo and Mohammedan inhabitants is indeed a subject of more than passing significance, but though a deep-seated difficulty, it is manifestly under effective control. The economic disturbance caused by the depreciation of silver and the recent closing of the

Indian mints to the further coinage of that metal, and the agitation for its remonitzation constitute the leading factors in the existing status of East Indian affairs.

FINIS.